"We're divi — why don't you say it?"

In answer Shan's eyes flashed fire. "All right. We are divided over your daughter. As long as she believes that her mother was some sort of goddess, she will never accept a mere mortal like me."

King's face contorted. "How can I tell her about her mother? It would destroy her."

"Isn't it that you won't tell her because it would mean admitting you made a mistake? And the cattle king never makes a mistake.... But it doesn't make much difference now. I still can't stay here. There's no future for us."

He stood profiled against the moonlit sky. "I gave you something you needed desperately—completeness. You've tasted it once, my darling, now you'll crave it forever. I'm an addiction."

Valerie Parv had a busy and successful career as a journalist and advertising copywriter before she began writing for Harlequin in 1982. She is an enthusiastic member of several Australian writers' organizations. Her many interests include her husband, her cat and the Australian environment. Her love of the land is a distinguishing feature in many of her books for Harlequin. She has recently written a colorful study in a nonfiction book titled *The Changing Face of Australia*. Her home is in New South Wales.

Books by Valerie Parv

HARLEQUIN ROMANCE

These books may be available at your local bookseller.

Return to Faraway

Valerie Parv

Harlequin Books

TORONTO • NEW YORK • LONDON
AMSTERDAM • PARIS • SYDNEY • HAMBURG
STOCKHOLM • ATHENS • TOKYO • MILAN

Original hardcover edition published in 1986
by Mills & Boon Limited

ISBN 0-373-02778-8

Harlequin Romance first edition July 1986

CHAPTER ONE

'THIRTY-THOUSAND dollars? But we could *buy* the place for that! I'll have to let you know later.'

Dispiritedly, Shan Penrose slammed the telephone down, unhappiness dulling the light in her piercing green eyes. Her downcast gaze rested on the doodles she'd drawn on her notepad—all dollar signs. 'Oh sh ... shivers!' What were they going to use for a location now?

'Did I hear our fearless leader using bad language?' came a cheerful voice and Shan's assistant, Rona Lawrence, breezed into the room.

Shan smiled wanly. 'It was a near thing. The cattle station people are asking thirty-thousand dollars to let us use their property for the outdoor sequences.'

Rona stared at her open-mouthed. 'They can't be serious. The whole property isn't worth that much.'

'That's what I said. I'm afraid they're very serious. Like most outsiders, they think all film people are rolling in money.'

Rona's answering smile was wry. 'If they could see our bank balance, they'd realise it's a miracle that *Call of the Outback* is being made at all.'

'That's assuming it still is,' Shan said gloomily.

'Oh, Shan, is there a chance it could be cancelled?'

'More than a chance—a distinct possibility. I had the bank manager on the 'phone again this morning. He reminded me that our grant from the Film Commission ran out long ago and threatened to start bouncing cheques if we didn't get this film into production like yesterday.'

5

Rona nodded in understanding. 'The bank won't part with any more money until the cameras are rolling, will they?'

Shan shook her head. 'And that can't happen until we find a suitable location . . . cheap.'

Rona grinned. 'I think this is where I came in.'

Decisively, Shan pushed the blotting paper with its accusing doodles away from her. 'Speaking of which . . .'

'Oh yes, I came in to tell you there's a young lady outside who wants to see you.'

Shan rolled her eyes upwards. 'Not another aspiring actress. Didn't you tell her the leads have all been cast?'

'Of course. But she insisted that you'd see her if I told you who it was.' She consulted her notepad. 'She says her name is Tammy Falconer.'

Shan's throat went dry and she gripped the edges of her desk convulsively. '*Who* did you say?' She'd heard Rona perfectly well but her mind refused to accept that her past had chosen such a dreadful time to rise up and confront her. Rona opened her mouth to repeat the name, but Shan waved her away. 'It's all right, I heard. The name just caught me by surprise.'

Rona's curiosity was clearly aroused. 'Who is the mysterious Miss Falconer?'

With great difficulty, Shan found her voice and framed the answer with parched lips. 'My . . . my stepdaughter.'

One of Rona's virtues was knowing when to speak and when to keep silent. From Shan's expression, she guessed that now was one of the latter times. She had known about Shan's ill-starred marriage, of course. Sharing the struggle to establish an independent production company, the two women had become close. But never once had Shan mentioned a child of the union. With an obvious effort, Rona stilled the myriad questions buzzing through her brain. 'Shall I show her in?'

Shan glanced around the room looking for some reason, anything, to delay facing Tammy although inwardly, she already knew she would have to go through with it. 'Yes, tell her I'll see her,' she said resignedly, then as Rona turned away, she added, 'No wait, give me five minutes before you bring her in.'

Rona gave her the 'thumbs up' signal. 'Five minutes, Miss Penrose.' In show business parlance, this meant five minutes to curtain-up—which wasn't far wrong to Shan's way of thinking.

In one corner of her office there was a hand basin with a cracked and spotted mirror over it. Shan darted to it and splashed cool water on to her face to tone down the hectic colour staining her cheeks. The effort was only partially successful so she reached for her make-up purse which lay on a shelf above the sink and went to work. A few minutes later, she felt calmer and hoped she looked a little better.

At twenty-four, she could still get by using only soap and water but occasionally as now, she relied on make-up as a disguise against the world. Examining herself critically in her mirror, she was thankful for the flaws in the glass which prevented her from studying herself too closely.

Her hair was undoubtedly her best feature. It was a lustrous dark brown which she occasionally high-lighted with a touch of henna. She made the most of her natural curls by wearing her hair in a mass of loose, pretty waves swept high off her face and kept in place by tortoise shell combs or, more often, a pair of sunglasses perched on her head.

Apart from that, her own judgment was that she was too short, although luckily she was trimly built to compensate, with legs which Rona said had no right to be so long and slender on someone so diminutive. Shan had long ago decided that her nose was crooked and her eyes too close together—a verdict hotly denied by everyone else who knew her, especially her male admirers. There were still a few, despite the fact that she had a failed marriage behind her, she thought ruefully.

Thinking of her marriage brought a wave of acute and quite unexpected pain. She had thought herself proof against it by now. Evidently her insouciance was only a veneer, if the mere mention of Tammy's name could pierce her emotional armour so easily. Why did she have to come here now?

'Miss Falconer,' Rona said formally from the doorway.

Shan whirled around as Rona showed a tall, slender teenager into her office. 'Tammy?' she asked quizzically.

The girl grinned disarmingly. 'Yes, it's me. I'll bet I don't look anything like the spoiled brat you remember?'

'No, you don't,' Shan said bluntly, thinking that she didn't sound much like it, either.

'I'll leave you two together,' Rona murmured tactfully and backed out of the room, closing the door behind her.

Alone with Tammy, at first Shan could only stare at the beauty time had brought out in the girl. She would be about eighteen now and the intervening three years had softened her once-angular lines into feminine curves. She was still reed-slim. Her fine blonde hair which fell to her shoulders was soft and wavy in front and cut away behind the ears into an intriguing elfin style. Only her eyes were the same as Shan remembered—hard and glittering with a painful echo of King about them. No! her mind screamed. She had promised herself she wouldn't think about him, but it was a struggle not to with his daughter sitting in front of her. She schooled her tone to sound conversational. 'What can I do for you, Tammy?'

The voice was as hard and the manner as calculating as ever. 'Actually, it was more what I could do for you,' Tammy said casually.

'What do you mean?'

Tammy riffled through her handbag and pulled out a newspaper clipping which Shan recognised as the publicity story she'd planted about the company's seach for a location. 'This is your company they're talking about?'

Shan nodded warily. 'Yes. We're looking for a property where we can film the outdoor sequences for *Call of the Outback*.'

'I've read the book,' Tammy confirmed. 'It should make a terrific film.'

'Obviously we think so. But I don't see . . .'

'You didn't think of asking Dad if you could use Faraway, did you?'

'Yes, I thought about it.' And not only for the film, but on a million other occasions when she was awake or asleep—had she thought about the ruggedly beautiful property in the Northern Territory where her hopes had been raised then cruelly dashed. But she didn't say this to Tammy, offering instead, 'Your father and I parted on such bad terms that I didn't think he would want me back on his property.'

Tammy's eyes glittered with satisfaction. 'Oh, but he does. He read the story of how you needed a cattle station and suggested that I talk to you about it.'

'He actually suggested your coming here?' Shan asked in astonishment.

'Better than that, he put it in writing.' She dipped

into her bag again and produced a typewritten letter on Faraway stationery.

Even before she took the note in her hands, Shan recognised the bold, scrawling signature across the bottom and her heart constricted at the sight of it. She forced her eyes to focus on the words.

'Dear Shan,' it read, 'I have been following your search for a suitable property on which to make your film and am surprised you haven't thought of using Faraway, which sounds ideal for your needs. In a sense, it is your home, or was until you decided otherwise.

'Tammy is delivering this letter from me in the hopes that you will consider the following proposition. Tammy aspires to becoming a professional actress. You wish to make a film in the Territory. If you can see your way to giving her a part in your production, then Faraway is at your disposal.

'I trust you will find my offer fair and worthy of your earnest consideration. Sincerely, King.'

How like King to want to use Shan's dilemma as a stepping stone for his daughter's career! Tammy—it had always been Tammy. Apparently, nothing had changed. Shan lifted her chin and her eyes met Tammy's. 'Thank your father for his offer, but tell him I am unable to accept.'

There was a brief flash of spirit in the younger girl's eyes, then she dropped her long lashes over them, curtaining her expression. Her voice was pitched low and filled with regret. 'I'll tell him when he gets back.'

'Gets back from where?' Shan asked in spite of herself.

'He's overseas on a cattle buying expedition. That's why he thought you'd be willing to consider his offer. By the time he returns, you'll be gone again.'

Shan felt a tremor of excitement surge through her. Surely if King wasn't going to be there, using Faraway would be no different from using any other cattle property—except that this one was being offered on a plate and without a thirty-thousand dollar price tag. 'Are you sure he won't be back?' she asked huskily.

Tammy frowned crossly. 'I just said so, didn't I?'

'I'm sorry, I didn't mean to imply anything,' Shan said, then realised how quickly she was falling back into the pattern of apologising to her stepdaughter. Everything was happening too fast. She needed time to think. 'Are you staying in Sydney?' she asked.

'Just overnight. I fly back to the Territory tomorrow.'

'Then leave me the number of your hotel and I'll ring you tomorrow with my answer.'

Tammy took the proffered pad and pen and wrote down a telephone number on it. 'I'll be there until noon,' she said, handing them back to Shan. 'Oh, you'll need this to help you make up your mind.' She passed a folder across the desk.

Shan recognised it as an actress's portfolio. She glanced through it. 'Very professional,' she murmured.

'Of course. I'm not just playing at this, you know.'

'I wasn't suggesting that you were. The problem is finding a suitable part in the film for you. Most of the casting is well advanced by now.'

Tammy smiled sweetly. 'I'm sure you'll think of something.'

It was only as she showed her stepdaughter out of the office that Shan realised how her last remark had betrayed her to Tammy. In her mind, she had already accepted King's offer. She had no choice and she had a feeling that Tammy knew it. If she didn't agree to use Faraway as a location, the film would have to be cancelled. With so many people depending on her, she would be heartbroken if it came to that. It would also mean the end of her dream of succeeding as a producer.

'Pizza time!' announced a cheerful voice from the doorway. She looked up to see Rona regarding her curiously. 'Everything all right?'

'Yes, fine. Look, you go ahead and have lunch. I've got some thinking to do.'

'Well, if you're sure?'

She nodded and Rona closed the door, her expression injured. It was the first time Shan had excluded her from a problem. But much as Shan hated hurting her loyal associate, this was one burden she didn't feel up to sharing. No one in the whole world, and especially not King Falconer, knew how desperately she still loved him. Returning to Faraway would be like twisting a knife in a wound which had only now begun to heal a little.

Their first meeting had given her no inkling of the pain which lay ahead with him. She had been eighteen then, the same age as Tammy was now. But there, any similarity ended. Where Tammy had led a spoilt, privileged existence, Shan had grown up in suburban Brisbane in a loving but very ordinary home.

With her parents' blessing, she had left school at sixteen to fulfil her dream of working in the film industry. By the time she was eighteen she had worked her way up the ladder to the job of continuity girl with a large production company. It was in this job that she first encountered King Falconer.

She would never forget the moment. The cast, headed by the well-known actress, Joanna Price, had been rehearsing a crucial scene, leaving Shan with nothing to do for the time being. Earlier, someone had pointed King out to her as Joanna's husband so she was not surprised to find him sitting on the sidelines watching the rehearsal.

'Enjoying yourself?' she asked conversationally.

'Not really,' was his unexpected answer. 'It all seems to move so slowly.'

'It may seem that way to an outsider, but I can assure you that progress is being made.' She went on to tell him how the actors' moves were choreographed as carefully as dance steps to provide all the required camera angles. She avoided mentioning that Joanna's fits of temperament meant everything took twice as long as it needed to.

As she talked she was unaware of the sparkle of enthusiasm which lit her green eyes or the glow which her pleasure in her work brought to her cheeks, until she realised that the man was studying her with an amused expression. 'I'm sorry. I didn't mean to go on at such length,' she said, embarassed.

'Don't apologise. You've brought the whole thing to life for me,' he said earnestly.

For the first time, she really looked at him, noting with breathless wonder how tall and broad shouldered he was—quite the biggest man she had ever met. But it wasn't his physical size which impressed her so much as his commanding presence, as if he was a man accustomed to giving orders and having them obeyed. His voice was like a glass of vintage burgundy, rich and full-bodied, she decided, then chided herself for being so fanciful. He was the star's husband and probably thought she had a cheek even chatting to him. 'I ... I'd better get back to work,' she murmured.

To her surprise, he grasped her arm. 'Don't go just yet,' he appealed. 'From what you've told me, there's nothing for you to do until they finish the rehearsal.'

'All right, I'll stay but just for a minute or two more.'

The minute or two had turned into half an hour during which she learned that he owned an immense cattle station in the Northern Territory.

'You're a long way from home,' she remarked.

'Yes, but I owe it to Joanna to take an interest in her work,' he said.

There had been a wistful note in his voice which tugged at Shan's heartstrings. It was apparent that he hated spending time away from his cherished property. She had to remind herself again that he was Joanna's husband and the actress might have been the model for the 'hell hath no fury' maxim. 'I really must get back to work,' she said firmly.

'Will I see you again later?' he asked.

It was extraordinarily difficult to give the answer she knew she must. 'I don't think so. Besides, Joanna can tell you anything more you want to know about the film business,' she said, then resolutely returned to her work.

He became a regular visitor to the set after that. He didn't appear to single Shan out but it was amazing how many times he contrived to be sitting on the sidelines where she was working, so she couldn't avoid talking to him. At other times, she was disturbingly aware of his eyes on her as she went about her work. She began to take extra care with her clothes and make-up, telling herself it had nothing to do with him. Nevertheless, she was unaccountably disappointed on the days when she couldn't spot him among the onlookers. She had never been so aware of a man as she was of King Falconer, and it was with mixed feelings that she greeted the end of that project.

It should have been the end of her fascination with him, too. A chance encounter, soon forgotten. Except that she hadn't been able to forget him so easily. During their short acquaintance, he had imprinted himself so indelibly upon her mind that, for months afterwards, she still found herself comparing other men to him. Most of them came off a poor second.

When, on the industry grapevine, she heard rumours that Joanna Price's marriage was on the rocks, her hopes began to soar until she reminded herself that rumours were two a penny in this business.

Then she had been offered a job as assistant producer on a film being made at Alice Springs in the Northern Territory. Even as she accepted the offer, telling herself that it was a step up in her career, she knew she was saying yes as much in the hope of seeing King Falconer again as for any other reason.

It seemed that she was not the only one who had been haunted by their meeting. The project at the Alice was just drawing to a close when he telephoned her at the motel.

'I heard you were in the vicinity and wondered if you remembered me?' he said diffidently.

Considering that 'the vicinity' was some twelve hundred kilometres away from his property, she was impressed, at the same time telling herself not to get carried away. 'Of course I remember you,' she told him, 'you're Joanna Price's husband.' This last was added for both their sakes, she told herself virtuously.

There was a long silence and she was afraid that her reminder of his married state had antagonised him, then he came back on the line. 'I wanted to talk to you about that, and about us.'

When did there get to be an 'us'? she thought in panic, aware that her pulses had begun to race alarmingly. 'Go on,' she said with a calmness she was far from feeling.

'Not like this, over the 'phone. I want you to come to Faraway. Please say you'll come, Shan?'

The caressing way he said her name brought the hairs erect on the back of her neck. She threw caution to the wind. 'I . . . I'd like that. I'll be finished here in about a week.'

'Then I'll send my plane for you in a week's time.'

They agreed on the time and place and she hung up feeling dazed. Whatever was she thinking of, agreeing to go to his property knowing perfectly well that he was committed to Joanna? Now that she thought about it, the industry grapevine had been unusually quiet on the subject for months so she had no idea whether the actress was even in Australia. Maybe she was making a film in another country, which might explain King's eagerness to invite Shan to his property.

Even as she argued and remonstrated with herself, she knew she would keep the rendezvous. Her behaviour was utterly unscrupulous, but where King was concerned, she had trouble remembering what a scruple was supposed to look like.

It was even harder when she met him again face to face. Her memory of their meeting two years ago hadn't exaggerated his good looks or his commanding presence. Here, on his own property, he looked like a hand inside a particularly well-fitting glove.

'Welcome to Faraway,' he said as he helped her down from the light plane on to the property's airstrip. His touch was fiery and his grip disturbingly possessive.

'Why is it called Faraway?' she asked in an attempt to disguise her feeling of awkwardness.

'Because when I bought it, my friends said it was too bloody far away.'

Their shared laughter eased the tension of the first moments together and she gradually relaxed in his company. He told her that the property covered eight hundred square miles. 'It covers some of the finest cattle grazing and in the Territory, and also some of the wildest country.'

Since the nearest town was Katherine, over fifty miles away, she could well believe it.

She didn't know what she expected of his home, but it certainly wasn't the impressive house he drove them to. Set on a raft of concrete, it was built of irregularly shaped stone quarried, King told her, from the site itself. The doors and windows were of western red cedar and the rest of the joinery was radiata pine and oregon so the house fitted naturally into its environment.

They entered the house from a wide verandah connecting the two wings of the house, with an open-ended courtyard in between. He showed her straight into the huge living room off which she glimpsed a kitchen. The other wing contained the bedrooms, she assumed.

Although it was early afternoon, he went straight to a bar straddling one end of the room. 'Brandy and soda?' he queried. She nodded, suddenly tongue tied. He handed her a glass then sat down opposite her, cradling his drink. 'You must be wondering why I asked you to come.'

'Good old country hospitality, I assumed,' she said fatuously.

His blue eyes met hers unflinchingly. 'I had to see you again. You may not believe this but I haven't been able to get you out of my mind since we met on the set of Joanna's film in Sydney.'

'I believe you because I feel the same way,' she confessed. 'I kept telling myself it was wrong, you were married . . .'

'But I'm not,' he interrupted harshly. 'Joanna's dead.'

She stared at him, the sorrow she knew she should

express for his bereavement battling with her own sudden inclination to laugh aloud. It was all right. He was a free man. Then she realised how callous this thought was. 'I'm sorry,' she said quietly and surprised herself by meaning it.

'Don't be. We were divorced long before she died, so there's nothing to be sorry about.'

So the rumours had been true, although he'd obviously managed to hush up most of the story. There hadn't been a whisper about Joanna's death in the gossip columns or even in the trades which usually relished such news. But now was hardly the time to press King for an explanation. 'You must have loved her once,' she said softly.

He stared moodily into his glass, making no move to drink. 'I did—once. I loved her passionately and I thought she felt the same way. Gradually, I realised that I was nothing more than an insurance policy in case her career ever failed her.'

Instinctively, she stretched out a hand to him. 'Oh, King, how terrible for you.'

He took her hand, gripping it convulsively so she had to grit her teeth against the pain, then he came to his senses and his hold slackened. 'Somehow I knew you'd understand. I guess that's why I wanted you to come here so badly.'

She grinned wryly. 'A shoulder to cry on?'

'If you thought that, you'd be on the next plane out of here.'

He was right. He wasn't the kind of man to want or need sympathy, so that wasn't why he had summoned her here. He had loved Joanna passionately, he said. A warm sensation seared the pit of her stomach. What would it be like to be the object of his passion? 'I'm glad you called me,' she said.

In three strides, he crossed the room and sat down

on the sofa beside her. Then with an oath, he pulled her into his arms. The drink she'd placed on the floor beside her was upended, the liquid disappeared instantly into the plush rug. But she paid it no heed, too intent was she on the surge of emotions which broke over her like a giant wave rolling on to the shoreline. His mouth was warm and firm, closing over hers possessively, while their bodies moulded into one line. She was on fire with a new and wonderful sensation and she wanted only to be consumed by him. Then, inexplicably, he pulled away from her, and half turned away. 'I'm sorry, I didn't mean to do that just yet.'

'Don't apologise,' she said breathlessly, the taste of him still strong on her lips. Her tongue moved restively over her mouth, savouring him. 'I didn't mind, honestly.'

'Then you won't mind if I do it again?' She shook her head. Never mind that true love was supposed to flower slowly, growing with time. By some strange alchemy, their love had been born in full bloom and she wanted to savour every sweet moment of it lest it wither as swiftly as it had blossomed.

In the two weeks which followed, their love showed no signs whatever of withering until, at King's urging, she cancelled her next assignment back in Sydney to stay on at Faraway.

She was dimly conscious that there were other people on the property, among them a housekeeper and a small army of station hands, both black and white, but she had eyes only for King.

Still, one thing puzzled her. Why had he made no attempt to come to her bed? She would have accepted him gladly, having long ago abandoned any pretence of prudence where he was concerned. It wasn't because he didn't want to make love to her, she could

swear. She knew that because his warm hands often
strayed inside her clothing when he kissed her with
feverish intensity. But he always pulled away at the
last minute.

When, yet again, his embraces left her flushed and
aching with unfulfilled longing, she could stand it no
longer. 'What's wrong with me, King?' she demanded.

He seemed startled by the question. 'Nothing's
wrong with you—why?'

'Then why don't you want to make love to me?'

He raked his fingers through his silver-flecked hair.
'I want to, God knows. But this time I have to be
sure.'

It was her turn to be baffled. 'Sure of what? That I
love you? You must know that I do, with all my heart.'

He regarded her levelly. 'I believe you and I believe
that you mean it—at this moment.'

'Then what . . .?'

He held up a hand, forestalling her. 'Let me finish.
Joanna swore she loved me and her life here at
Faraway. But it didn't take her long to tire of the
isolation and start yearning for her bright lights. I
have to be sure that won't happen again.'

She was nonplussed. 'I can't give you a lifetime
guarantee of happiness. Nobody can.'

'I'm not asking for one. I want you to be my wife
more than anything in the world, but there must be
conditions.'

'I'm listening,' she whispered.

'After we're married, I propose a trial period of, say,
three months, before we live together as man and wife.
You can back out of the arrangement any time during
that period and still have the benefit of my name and
property. Without any physical commitment, you
could have the marriage annulled if you preferred.'

Three months of knowing she was his wife but

unable to share his bed! It sounded like a new and exquisite form of torture. 'But why get married at all?' she asked unhappily. 'Why not just carry on as we are until you're sure of me?'

He stood up and began to pace up and down the room like a caged tiger. 'There's a reason why we have to be married. You see, I have a daughter, Tamara. When Joanna and I broke up, she tried to commit suicide. I can't risk giving her a new mother and having the same thing happen again. And she's much too impressionable for us just to live together.'

So stunned was she by this revelation that Shan had trouble taking it in. She had seen no signs of a child in the house. Granted, she hadn't explored all the bedrooms but surely there would have been something—photographs or childish books, anything—to tip her off. Unless King had deliberately hidden every clue. 'Why didn't you tell me you had a child?'

'I didn't want anything to spoil the last few weeks. They've been the happiest of my life. I ... I was afraid if you knew, it would change things between us.'

'Well of course it does, but not necessarily for the worst. How old is she? Where is she now?'

He held up a hand, his eyes bright with tears of happiness and relief at her response. 'Tamara ... that is, Tammy ... is fifteen and she's at boarding school in Adelaide at present. I was hoping you'd agree to have the wedding in three weeks' time when she comes home for the school holidays.'

He stood before her so uncertainly that her heart went out to him. He had been hurt so badly by Joanna that he was willing to forgo the physical pleasures of marriage until they were both certain of their decision. Tammy had also been hurt by her mother's desertion to the point of attempting to kill herself. Shan knew

King would get around to telling her the whole story in his own time. For now it was enough that they needed Shan to heal those wounds. Impulsively, she wound her arms around his shoulders, although she had to reach up a good foot to do so. 'Of course we'll get married then,' she assured him.

'Then you agree to the three-month trial?'

'Yes,' she said reluctantly, knowing instinctively that he would not be swayed on this point. 'But you said conditions, plural.'

'Joanna was always torn between her life with me, and her film career. I think it was that, more than anything, which destroyed our marriage. Eventually, the lure of filming was too strong and she spent more and more time away from us. Ironically, the glamour finally destroyed her—too many parties, too much drinking.'

'If you're asking me to choose between my work and marrying you, there's no contest,' Shan said at once. 'I love you and I love Faraway. How could I ever need anything more?'

'Tell me again in three months' time,' he said gruffly but she could see he was moved by her voluntary response.

'Does Tammy know about us?' she asked.

'I've written and told her how wonderful you are. She can't wait to get home and meet you.'

'I'm sure we'll all be very happy together,' Shan said, her eyes shining.

If only she could have known how wrong she would prove to be.

CHAPTER TWO

THE 'phone's insistent ringing interrupted Shan's reverie and she stared at the instrument for a few minutes, disorientated, still held in thrall by the flood of memories. Distantly she realised that she should answer the 'phone. 'Shan Falc ... er ... Penrose,' she muttered, then came back to the present with a jolt.

'Oliver Mortenson here, Miss Penrose.'

Her heart sank. She had forgotten she was supposed to call the bank manager with some sort of answer. 'Hello, Mr Mortenson. Sorry I haven't had a chance to call you back. I've been tied up with the problem of finding a location so the film can go ahead.' Which was true enough in its way, she supposed.

He sniffed audibly. 'I see. And what progress have you made?'

She knew he expected her to say none. He had made it quite clear that he disapproved of women in business and only his bank's equal opportunity policy had induced him to get involved with her company at all. He would take a fiendish delight in closing the production down. Well, she was damned if she'd give him that satisfaction, putting all the people who depended upon her out of work. 'I've found a splendid location.' There, her bridges were burned with a vengeance.

She could visualise his eyebrows arching in surprise. 'Really? And at what cost, may I ask?'

'None. A ... a relative of mine has offered us free use of his cattle station in the Northern Territory.'

'You wouldn't care to tell me the name of this . . . relative?' he asked, his tone frankly disbelieving.

'Mr King Falconer.' She stumbled slightly over the name. It was so long since she'd said it aloud.

There was a long pause. 'You mean the Cattle King himself is taking an interest in your project.'

'I suppose that is how he's commonly known,' she dissembled.

She could almost hear the bank manager's attitude start to mellow. 'Well, well, why didn't you say so before? Having Mr Falconer involved puts a different complexion on things.'

'Because he's male or because he's rich?' she asked acidly, forgetting momentarily how much the project depended on keeping the bank manager on their side.

He chose to gloss over her sarcasm. 'I can see you have the wrong impression of me, Miss Penrose. I have nothing against women in business . . .'

Provided they have wealthy male benefactors, she thought sourly but this time managed to keep the thought to herself. 'It's all right, Mr Mortenson,' she said tiredly, 'I'm glad you're happy with the new arrangements.'

'Of course, of course,' he said airily. 'With Mr Falconer as your backer . . .'

'I didn't say he was backing the film, only providing the location,' she interjected.

'All in good time, of course. Mustn't rush things, must we? But tell me, when do you start filming at the new location?'

'Almost immediately. I know you don't want the project held up any longer.'

'Of course not,' he soothed. 'Keep me posted, won't you?'

Men! she thought viciously as she set the 'phone down. She'd done it now. She was committed to going to Faraway whether she liked it or not. She wondered what the bank manager would have said if she'd told him she was the Cattle King's wife.

It was the truth, after all. Neither she nor King had got around to filing for divorce although their marriage had ended, as far as she was concerned, when he chose to believe Tammy instead of his own wife.

Their marriage had started off well enough even though King kept his vow to make it a union in name only for the first three months. The time would soon pass and they could share a bed as man and wife, she told herself as she lay achingly alone on what should have been her wedding night.

Nevertheless, it wasn't easy to convince herself of the necessity for such a condition. To Shan, a marriage was a union of minds as well as bodies. King might think that as long as they hadn't slept together, they weren't truly married but she knew she was wholly committed to him from the moment she made her vows in front of the minister who travelled out from Katherine to perform the ceremony.

So it was the sweetest torment to watch him go about his work on the property, muscles rippling from his exertions, and sweat glistening on his bare torso like salty tears. How she longed to stroke her hand down the length of his spine, feeling each separate vertebra under her fingers. She fantasised about massaging his wide shoulders until the knotted muscles relaxed in response to her ministrations.

'You're acting like a sex-starved old maid,' she told herself crossly but the more they were together, the more she longed for his fulfilment. It gnawed at her like an insatiable hunger. When he kissed her, it was like squeezing drops of water from a sponge on to the tongue of someone who was dying of thirst. Finally, she told herself to stop being so melodramatic. Three months wasn't forever. It would soon be over and they would be married in every sense of the word.

She had been unable to dismiss Tammy's reaction to their marriage so lightly. From the moment she arrived home from boarding school, it was obvious that she resented Shan's presence in her home.

At first, Shan did her utmost to be forbearing, telling herself that she was a stranger, and Tammy still bore the emotional scars from the break-up of her family. But everything came to a head one day when King had left them alone together while he supervised a dawn-to-dusk muster.

Shan made an effort to draw the younger girl out on fashion, music and current affairs, trying to find a common area of interest, but Tammy rebuffed her at every turn. At last, she said, 'Well what *do* you want to talk about, Tammy?'

'Frankly I have nothing to discuss with a woman like you,' she said archly.

Aware that she had paled under her sun tan, Shan fought for self-control. On how she reacted now, depended the future of her relationship with her stepdaughter. 'You seem to know a lot about me, considering we've hardly spoken,' she said with forced lightness.

'Oh, I know more about you than you think. You're the other woman.'

'Tammy! You don't know what you're talking about!'

'Don't I?' the teenager flashed back. 'I know you were responsible for breaking up my parents' marriage.'

'Where did you get such an idea?' Shan asked, shocked.

'From my mother. Oh, she and Dad had their differences, I know. But she was an artist—they're allowed to be temperamental, she always said. But they would have patched things up, I know they would, if *you* hadn't come along.'

'Just a minute, Tammy. There was nothing between your father and I before I came to the Territory, so I couldn't have had anything to do with the divorce.'

For a brief moment, uncertainty flickered across Tammy's young face. 'You mean you didn't know Dad before this?'

'Well, we met in Sydney, on the set of one of your mother's films, but . . .'

'I knew it! Mother knew it too. She said she could sense there was someone else, although Dad denied it. It was you all along.'

Too stunned at first to defend herself, Shan looked in horror at the teenager whose eyes had begun to brim with tears. In truth, she and King hadn't seen each other beyond those casual encounters on the set. But King had admitted he was unable to stop thinking about her. Was there such a thing as mental adultery? Had she unwittingly come between King and Joanna?

It was a painful thought. But no, she couldn't believe it of King. She already knew enough about him to know he was unswervingly loyal. He had fought for his marriage until all hope was gone, and he had fought for his daughter's wellbeing. There was no way he would have allowed a passing attraction such as theirs to jeopardise his family life. 'You're wrong, Tammy,' she said with conviction. 'There was nothing between your father and I while he was married to Joanna. You have to believe it.'

'And if I don't choose to?'

'Then there's nothing I can do to convince you. But I do want to be friends with you, if you'll let me. Your father wants it, too.'

'Oh, I know what my father wants,' Tammy shot

back cockily. 'The same thing all men want.' As Shan's eyebrows lifted in shock, she went on, 'Yes, I know he doesn't want you to sleep together until you're sure of each other, but don't you see? He wants to get you panting for it, then you'll give him anything he wants. For God's sake, Shan, you can't think you're his first "trial marriage"?'

'That's enough, Tammy!' Shan said coldly, putting all the authority she could muster into her voice. 'Your father's past is no concern of mine—or yours for that matter.'

Tammy's expression grew sly. 'What makes you think I was talking about the past?'

Shan had walked away then, afraid that her control would snap all together if she had to face that smug look for a moment longer. Behind her, she heard Tammy's mocking laughter following her.

She told herself that Tammy was speaking out of fear that her father's love was being stolen from her. Since she had lost her mother not long ago, in tragic circumstances, it was understandable that Tammy felt more than usually vulnerable and possessive towards her remaining parent. Shan didn't—couldn't—believe that she was only the latest in a string of trial marriages. She knew King better than to believe such a thing.

And yet, how much did she know about him? She had believed she knew him well but he had kept from her the existence of his teenage daughter. What else might he have concealed from her?

'No, I refuse to think like this,' she told herself determinedly. It was just what Tammy wanted her to think. By deliberately sowing suspicion in Shan's mind, she hoped to undermine her relationship with King. The ploy had no chance of succeeding as long as Shan held fast to her belief in King and in their love.

But what was she to do about Tammy's crazy idea that she had come between King and Joanna? There was no truth in the assertion, but as long as Tammy believed there was, they had no chance of becoming friends the way King wanted them to be. Since she couldn't convince Tammy she was wrong, Shan decided to be even more loving and tolerant towards the child to see if it made any difference.

It seemed as if no amount of love and tolerance was going to change Tammy's attitude. If anything, Shan's efforts to win her over only made her more arrogant and contemptuous of everything Shan tried to do for her. Once, she even said openly that it was only a matter of time before Shan left and Tammy took her rightful place as mistress of Faraway.

Shan could have consulted King about Tammy's behaviour but she was afraid he would think she was unable to cope with the child on her own. Besides which, she noticed that Tammy was never rude or challenging when King was around.

By careful probing, Shan discovered from King that Tammy hadn't wanted to live at Faraway at all after the divorce. Despite King's attempts to reason with her, she had asked the courts to allow her to live with her mother, Joanna Price. It had taken all of King's powers of persuasion to convince the authorites that Joanna was an unfit mother. She had been drinking heavily then and had continued after the divorce until she eventually drank herself to death, proving King tragically right.

Following her mother's death, Tammy had become increasingly withdrawn and difficult, culminating in her taking a bottle of her mother's sleeping pills. Only by a miracle had she been discovered in time.

After the suicide attempt, King heeded medical advice and sent Tammy away to boarding school in another state, hoping that time and a neutral environment would improve matters.

Tammy's apparent change of heart on her return this time had delighted him. He wasn't to know that it was brought about because she thought she was returning as mistress of Faraway. Finding a stranger in this position had awakened all her dormant bitterness and she had no scruples about taking it out on Shan.

If Tammy was seeking revenge on King for divorcing her adored mother, she couldn't have chosen a more effective course. She knew Shan loved King too much to tell him the real reason why their marriage wasn't working. If it failed, he would suffer agonies of torment, believing it was his fault. Tammy would assume her place as mistress of Faraway and would no doubt make sure that she was the only woman in King's life from then on.

It was a masterful plan, Shan had to concede. King already felt guilty enough over Tammy's attempted suicide, so he would never risk jeopardising her happiness again. With such a weapon at her disposal, was it any wonder that Tammy used it to the full?

Inevitably, despite her efforts to prevent it, the strain had begun to affect her relationship with King. He was fully occupied with an attempt to domesticate some of the fifteen-thousand or so head of water buffalo which ranged over the swampy reaches of the property. Many cattle men before him had tried and failed, but he was determined to succeed, believing that the animals—which were domestic in origin—could be tamed, mustered and shipped for export like ordinary cattle. His progress was evidenced by the thousand head of buffalo which were already grazing on irrigated Townsville lucerne near the homestead. But it was still gruelling and dangerous work and he returned sweat-soaked and burned to a dark mahogany after each long day in the harsh Territory sun.

Shan could understand why he was in no mood to be greeted by a strained, white-faced wife each evening, but she was unable to stop herself taking out her frustration with Tammy on the only available target, which happened to be King.

'For goodness sake, what's eating you this time?' he flared after yet another evening during which she'd answered him in monosyllables. 'It's me, isn't it? You're fed up with spending each day here miles from anywhere while I play cowboy, isn't that so?'

'No! It's nothing like that. I love *Faraway* . . . and you.'

'Then what is it?' he asked gruffly.

How could she tell him that the daughter he idolised, who behaved so charmingly in his presence, turned into a gutter-tongued monster by day? To King, Tammy was an innocent child who would have been shocked to find her father living with a woman out of wedlock. In truth, he was the one who would have been shocked if he knew that, thanks to Joanna's example, his daughter was tough and worldly wise beyond her years. 'Nothing's the matter,' she insisted.

'The hell there isn't. You've been growing more and more morose by the day. I can't believe such a change has happened without a cause.'

'I'm just tired, probably from spending too much time out in the sun,' she offered.

'Then all I can say is, you must be spending a lot of time in the sun on a lot of days,' was his churlish response.

They said nothing more to each other as the clock hands crawled agonisingly around to bedtime. At last Shan stood up and announced that she was going to bed. He merely nodded, making no attempt to kiss her good-night as he usually did.

Alone in her room, she stared unseeingly out of the window. If only he would end this farcical touch-me-not arrangement between them she was sure things would improve. But every time she brought it up, he reminded her of their agreement. And as long as Tammy knew they weren't sleeping together she would go on doing everything in her power to drive them apart.

Not for the first time, Shan thought about the letter in her dresser drawer. It was from a former colleague, Dave Cameron, telling her of an opening on a film he was involved with. Mindful of her promise to King, she had crumpled the letter up, then on impulse, had smoothed it out and slipped it into the drawer. She and Dave had grown up in the film business together. He at least deserved the courtesy of a polite refusal. The way things were between her and King, it was tempting to reconsider.

A cloud drifted away from the moon, throwing the garden into sharp relief and dappling the figure of a man which one of the aboriginal stockmen had carved from the living rock which stood there. The figure gave her an idea. King might be a man of iron control but *he* wasn't made of stone.

In a flurry of activity, she showered and took out a sheer, lace-trimmed nightie she'd bought for her trousseau, then slipped it over her shower-dewed skin. Then she brushed her hair into a fluffy halo around her shoulders and dashed cologne on to her pulse points, before setting off bare-footed down the corridor towards King's room.

There was a light under his door. Good, he was still awake. Her heart was pounding and there was a roaring sound in her ears as she reached for the doorknob. She pushed the door open a crack only to freeze as she heard voices coming from inside.

Through the crack she glimpsed Tammy clad in baby-doll pyjamas, perched cross-legged on her father's bed as she regaled him with gossip. Neither of them noticed as Shan eased the door shut again.

So much for her great seduction scene, she thought miserably. King was too preoccupied with his doting daughter to care whether or not his wife cried herself to sleep—which she did as soon as she was safely back in her own room.

Next morning she was red-eyed and lethargic when she came down for breakfast. King was alone for once and informed her that Tammy had gone for an early-morning ride. 'I'm glad we're alone. I've been wanting to talk to you about her,' Shan said hesitantly.

His face took on a strained look. 'I had a feeling this was coming on, but let's hear it anyway.'

'I'm afraid she doesn't like me.'

'That's arrant nonsense,' he exploded. 'She thinks you're wonderful. She told me so herself last night. It's she who's upset because you don't like her, despite her best efforts to win you over.'

The room began to swim around Shan and she placed both hands flat on the table to steady herself. 'Is that what she told you?' He nodded grimly. 'Well it isn't true. She's been intolerably rude to me ever since she came home. King, she won't be happy until she's driven us apart—can't you see that?'

His expression remained impassive. 'She warned me you'd say something like that. She has tried very hard to get along with you, Shan, because she knows what it means to me. She also knows that I place her happiness ahead of my own. After what she went through when Joanna and I split up, I owe her that much.'

Her voice was vibrant with emotion. 'And what about what we owe each other?'

'You and I don't owe each other anything,' he reminded her tersely. 'That was the whole point of the trial period—so that either of us could walk away unscathed if it didn't work out.'

'Is that what you want to do—walk away?' she asked, her voice rising.

'No. But I was wondering if it was what you wanted to do.'

She was stunned. 'Whatever makes you think that?'

'Aren't you thinking of going back to work with your film friends? You can't deny you've had offers?'

How on earth had he found out about Dave's letter? 'Yes, I've had *one* offer.' She emphasised the number. 'How did you find out?'

'I found the letter lying on your bed where you left it.'

Leaving aside why he might have come to her room, which hurt too much to think about at present, she knew she hadn't left the letter lying around. She distinctly remembered pushing it into her dresser drawer. Only one person would have pried into her things like that, and left the letter where King could find it. But if she said as much, King would only think it was further evidence of her antipathy towards Tammy.

He drummed his fingers in an irritable tattoo on the tablecloth. 'Well? What are you going to do about the offer?'

Why didn't he tell her how much he needed her and say that he wanted her to stay? It was as if he *wanted* their marriage to fail to reaffirm his belief that the film world was a corrupting influence. Did he need that to be able to live with the memory of Joanna's desertion?

'I ... I'll tell you my decision later when I've had some time to think,' she said, surprising herself. She had believed that there was no decision to make.

'Will you now? That's very generous of you,' he sneered, then his tone changed suddenly to one of appeal. 'Can't you see, Shan? It's this very uncertainty I was afraid of. You seemed so sure that this was the life you wanted. What changed everything?'

Your daughter, she could have answered but bit back the words. Even if he sided with her now, he would end up hating her for coming between him and Tammy. 'Nothing's changed, King. I just need some time to think things over.'

'Then you *were* thinking of going away.' She started to protest but he silenced her with a thunderous look. 'Don't bother to rationalise it, I've heard it all before. Maybe it's just as well you and Tammy didn't hit it off. I shudder to think what might have happened if she'd become attached to you and then you let her down.'

He stood up so abruptly that his chair crashed to the floor. Ignoring it, he stormed out and she heard the screen door slam behind him.

For a long time, she remained at the table staring at the debris of her uneaten breakfast. So his insistence on a trial marriage had been as much to ensure that Tammy approved of her as to ensure that she could handle station life.

As if in a dream, she got to her feet, sure of what she had to do next. There was no way she could compete with a woman who had a fifteen-year head start on her, as Tammy had. And teenager or not, she was worldly enough to be called a woman. How she would gloat when she found that she had won. Resolutely, Shan fetched Dave's letter and 'phoned through her acceptance of his job offer by telegram.

Even though it had happened three years ago now, Shan still remembered every detail of her flight from Faraway. She had packed quickly, wanting to be clear

of the homestead before Tammy returned from her
ride. Then she had called the airport at Katherine and
booked a seat on the only available flight south. To
avoid arousing curiosity, she had borrowed one of the
station's four-wheel-drive vehicles and driven herself
to the airport, barely making it in time for the flight.
She had abandoned the car at the airport with a note
under the windshield wiper, knowing it would soon be
found and reported to King.

For a long time, she had expected him to come after
her or at least to try to contact her. But months passed
and no word came. Her letters to him remained
unanswered and finally, she accepted that he meant it
when he said he placed Tammy's happiness ahead of
his own. Apparently, Shan's feelings didn't come into
it at all.

To fill the yawning chasm he had left in her life, she
threw herself into her career and worked with a will
which left her colleagues bemused, but which brought
her one assignment after another. Each one took her a
little higher up the promotional ladder.

Her dream of starting her own production company
had eluded her, however, until she submitted the
latest of many applications for development funding to
the Australian Film Commission. To her joy, the
grant was forthcoming, enabling her to buy the rights
to the Australian classic, *Call of the Outback* and set
about developing it into a film. Despite meticulous
budgeting, her funds had run out a month ago and her
entreaties to the A.F.C. for further funding had so far
met with encouragement, but no success. The bank
was now her only hope.

Now her dream had a chance of being fulfilled, but
at what cost? Even knowing that King wouldn't be
there, could she go back to Faraway knowing what it
meant to her, and do her job as if nothing was amiss?

'Yes, damn it, I can,' she vowed.

She was unaware of having spoken aloud until Rona stuck her head around the door. 'Can what?'

'I was doing a bit of positive thinking. Telling myself we can get this film made.'

Rona grinned. 'What rabbit have you pulled out of the hat now?'

Shan filled her in on the meeting with Tammy, explaining about the offer but leaving out her own feelings about going back to Faraway. 'It's blackmail, but we'll have to find her a part somehow,' she concluded.

Rona had been thumbing through Tammy's portfolio. 'According to this, she's had some useful experience in TV commercials and modelling work in Darwin and Adelaide. She certainly looks angelic.'

How deceiving looks can be, Shan thought uncharitably. 'Casting's more your area than mine—what do you think?'

'How about we try her as Libby, the daughter of the station owner?'

'Appropriate enough, and not too many lines for a relative newcomer. But didn't you have someone in mind for that?'

'There is a young actress I was hoping to get, but we haven't signed her yet.'

'She'll be disappointed,' mused Shan.

'It's either her or the bank manager.'

'Then it looks as if we have ourselves an actress,' Shan said decisively.

'And a location—thank the Lord!' added Rona.

In spite of her determination to treat this purely as a business decision, Shan couldn't summon up the same fervour. She felt nothing but trepidation at the prospect of going back to Faraway. Even though she wouldn't have to face King, there was no way she could avoid facing her memories.

CHAPTER THREE

A WEEK later the company flew into Katherine during what was supposed to be the northern mid-winter, but it was many degrees hotter than the southern states they had left behind.

Rona mopped her brow theatrically. 'This is winter? What must summer be like?'

'There isn't one,' laughed Shan. 'There are only two seasons up here—the Wet and the Dry. You can thank your lucky stars this is the Dry.'

'Is the Wet as bad as it sounds?'

'Worse! We probably wouldn't be able to reach the homestead in the Wet. Most of the surrounding plains would be under water. For that matter, so would we. It rains almost non-stop for the whole season.'

Rona looked nervously up at the sky which was an innocent pale blue. 'Shouldn't we get moving?'

'Relax. It won't start raining for months yet. We have plenty of time.' But even as she reassured her associate, Shan was anxious to complete the location shooting herself, although for quite different reasons. The sooner they got to Faraway, the sooner she would be finished there. She wanted to be long gone by the time King returned.

As it was, every mile of the way through the neat township of Katherine and along the Stuart Highway to the turnoff for Faraway was steeped in bittersweet memories. The sight of the reddish brown cliffs bordering the cool green Katherine River brought a lump to her throat. How well she remembered boating down the Gorge with King. He had pointed out the cascading greenery and palms growing out of the sheer rock face, explaining that they were sustained by water stored at the top of the cliffs in the Wet. Now, during the Dry, the water seeped through the rock and tumbled in sparkling rivulets down the rock face. It was so beautiful it almost hurt to look at it.

'What a setting!' enthused Rona. Her comment was echoed by the rest of the company travelling in a convoy of four-wheel-drive vehicles. 'It's absolutely perfect for our needs.'

Looking at the lush tropical setting which was so in contrast to the arid plains not far to the south and west, Shan wondered how she could have thought of filming anywhere else. The road followed the slow-flowing green river for some miles and there was great excitement when someone spotted a Johnson River crocodile basking on a log at the water's edge.

'I'm glad we're insured in case anybody gets eaten,' her old friend, Dave Cameron observed. He had joined Shan's company as the film's director and she was grateful for his good humoured support.

'Luckily, they don't eat people,' Shan assured him. 'It's the salties—the saltwater crocs—you need to watch out for. They have a shorter, stubbier snout than the Johnson River variety.'

Dave shot her a sceptical glance. 'Remind me to measure the noses of any crocodiles we meet while we're filming.'

Everyone was in good spirits by the time they reached the homestead, although they were all hot and thirsty and caked in the superfine reddish dust which was characteristic of the Territory.

The only one who didn't join in the party mood was Shan. Her nerves stretched to near-breaking point as they neared the homestead. Even knowing that King wouldn't be there, she still resisted the idea of

returning. She had left part of herself behind here—
the warm, caring part which was capable of loving a
man. It had been trampled in the dust because of that
man's indifference to her feelings. Whatever she told
herself, she wasn't yet ready to revisit the shrine of her
destruction.

But the cars had pulled up outside the low stone
building and someone was waving to them from the
front verandah, so there was nothing for it but to
climb stiffly out of the car.

'Shan—how marvellous to see you!' She tensed as a
middle-aged woman in a flowered apron came rushing
out to greet her.

'How are you, Mrs Gordon? It's nice to see you
again,' she responded, forcing herself to smile. King's
housekeeper had shown her nothing but kindness
during her previous stay here. It wouldn't be fair to
take her tension out on the housekeeper.

'Tammy told you how many of us were coming?'
she asked.

A frown creased Mrs Gordon's forehead. 'Yes, for a
wonder. Her visitors usually just arrive out of the blue
and she expects me to cater for them at a moment's
notice. I think she enjoys lording it over me now
there's no one to stop her. It was a pity for all our
sakes that you went away, Shan.'

'I didn't have much choice,' Shan said quickly. Of
the rest of the company, only Rona knew that she had
been married to King Falconer and even she didn't
know the whole story. As far as the others knew, he
was a distant relative of Shan's who had kindly let
them use his property, so she didn't want the
housekeeper to give her secret away. She made a
mental note to caution Mrs Gordon as soon as she got
the chance. 'What arrangements have you made for
us?' she asked to distract her for the moment.

'I've put you all in the guest quarters,' Mrs Gordon told her, 'And you've got your old room in the homestead, Shan.'

'Oh no thank you, I'd rather stay with the others.' The last thing she wanted was to spend her nights under King's roof. As Mrs Gordon's face fell, she added, 'It's better that way. If we need to work late, I won't have to disturb anyone.'

To her relief, the housekeeper accepted her improvised explanation. 'I suppose that makes sense. I'll have another room made up for you in the guest quarters then.'

Like many of the properties in the area, Faraway had been established in the 1800s as a sheep station until the land proved to be unsuitable for sheep. The guest quarters had been created out of the old shearing shed which was now so transformed as to be unrecognisable.

Inside the two-storey stone outbuilding, a series of small but comfortable single rooms had been created with a bathroom servicing each pair of rooms. Shan had warned everyone not to expect luxurious accommodation and most of the company pronounced themselves happy with the arrangements.

Only one man began to complain about sharing a bathroom and Shan's spirits plummetted. Trust Jason Cody to be the one to complain. He played the leading role of the station owner in the film. How could anybody look so masculine and act so childishly?

'Did you hear me, Shan?' he repeated.

Everyone in the building had heard him! 'Yes, I know, you're unhappy because you have to share a bathroom, Jason. What would you suggest I do about it—have one built?'

'Well, no—I wouldn't go that far. But rest assured I'll be talking to my agent about this.'

Add it to the list, she thought mutinously, but avoided voicing the thought. Jason was being difficult enough as it was without giving him further ammunition. If only he wasn't such a good actor, Shan would never have put up with his outbursts of temperament but there was no denying he was perfect for the role. And he had been willing to undertake it for a very reasonable fee plus a percentage of any profits the film made when it was released.

Shan was well aware that Jason fancied her but she was convinced it was only because she was so resistant to his advances. He was accustomed to his star status bringing every woman he desired within his clutches so she was a novelty. It was the lure of the unattainable, and she would remain unattainable, especially when he carried on like this, she told herself.

'Maybe I can arrange for you to sleep at the homestead,' she said to soothe him.

'I knew you'd think of something.' He smiled and planted a kiss on her cheek before she could dodge him.

Since Mrs Gordon had prepared a room for her at the main house, it was a simple matter to arrange for Jason to use it. An *en suite* bathroom opened off the room so she knew it would make the star happy.

When he had inspected the room and pronounced it adequate, the housekeeper was beside herself with excitement. 'Imagine having Jason Cody sleeping under my roof,' she marvelled.

Her adoration came as no surprise to Shan. It was precisely for his appeal to a certain type of middle-aged woman that Jason got parts so readily. He was what was termed 'good box-office' and Shan was grateful for his presence in the film even if she had a hard time convincing him he didn't rate a place in her bed as a fringe benefit.

Soothing Jason's ruffled feathers was just one of the dozens of small tasks she was faced with before the company was settled at Faraway. Although she had Dave Cameron and Rona to assist her, she was still called on to make dozens of decisions about everything from shooting scripts to what sort of filling would be acceptable for the crew's lunchbox sandwiches.

She accepted every task gratefully to stop herself from thinking about King, but still his image haunted her everywhere she went on the property.

Most poignant of all was the sense of his presence when they filmed at the billabong some distance from the homestead. It was one of the first places to which King had brought her, to show her the wonders of the aboriginal cave paintings thousands of years old, which adorned the prehistoric strata.

King had kissed her here, his tongue exploring the moist cavern of her mouth as they had earlier explored the caves for treasure. In his kiss, she had found treasure of a sort in a wave of such longing for him that she was shaken when he released her. He had nearly broken his vow not to make love to her. If only he had, how different things might be between them now!

'Like to take a look at this, Shan?'

'What? Oh yes, John. I'll be right there.' Still drugged by her body's memories she moved stiffly to where the cameraman was waiting for her. She looked through the viewfinder and pronounced herself satisfied with the way the shot was framed.

Tammy had been made up as Libby, the teenage daughter of the station owner. The scene was a testing one for her because she was required to act out a love scene with a young aboriginal boy to whom she was attracted. Yet neither of them spoke the other's language so every emotion had to be expressed in pantomime.

Since there was no dialogue, the scene called for a good deal of acting skill. Before the astonished eyes of the crew, Tammy shed her spoiled rich-girl image and became a shy, simple teenager caught up in the wonder of her first love. She even managed to convey the tension underlying the romance, which both her family and the boy's tribe objected to.

When Dave called 'Cut!' there was spontaneous applause from the rest of the cast and crew, one of the greatest compliments they could pay to a fellow actor.

'She's dynamite,' Dave whispered to Shan. 'Wait till we get her and Cody on the screen together.'

'It will be interesting to see which ego comes out ahead,' Shan said drily, earning a curious look from Dave. Inwardly, she was relieved that Tammy's acting skills were equal to the job. Making a film on a shoestring was tough enough without running overtime because one of the actors needed constant direction. She sighed deeply. Why couldn't she just admit that Tammy was good? Her part in Shan's estrangement from King had nothing to do with this, surely.

Getting the billabong scene right from all the angles they needed took up most of the day. By the time Shan called it a wrap, they were all mentally and physically exhausted.

It was an effort even to drag herself up the stairs of the guest quarters. Only the thought of a cool shower spurred her on. She almost cried with annoyance when she found that someone had beaten her to their shared shower. 'Won't be long!' came Rona's singsong voice from inside.

Resigned to waiting her turn, she pushed open the door of her own room then went rigid as her nostrils were assailed by an all-too-familiar blend of spicy after-shave lotion and pure maleness.

'Hello, Shan,' King said quietly.

Like a cornered animal, she hunted the small room for somewhere to hide. Sensing her urge to flee, King sprang up and closed the door behind her then leaned casually against it. 'You seem to make a habit of running away from me.'

She found her voice with an effort. 'I wasn't expecting to see you, King.'

'I gathered that. How else would you have had the temerity to bring your people here, knowing how I feel about the film business.'

If he had hit her with a machete, she couldn't have been more stunned. 'I came here because you invited me,' she said coldly.

His mouth twisted into a parody of a smile. 'You of all people should know that the film business broke up both my marriages. That's hardly likely to make me into a fan.'

She couldn't believe she was hearing this. It was like her worst nightmares come to life. Desperately, she fought for calmness. 'I was surprised that you wanted me here but the only reason I would have agreed to come was by your invitation.'

He spread his hands wide. 'I assure you I issued no such invitation.'

Self-control deserted her. 'You did, I have your letter here!' Frantically she dug into her luggage, throwing clothes aside in her search. 'It was here, I swear.'

'Another of your fantasies?' he asked sardonically as the letter continued to elude her.

'I must have misplaced it. You wrote inviting me to use Faraway as a location in return for casting Tammy in the film.'

'Which would make sense if she was an actress.'

'You mean you didn't know she had taken up acting?'

'I knew she was doing a secretarial course in Adelaide. Shorthand and typing hardly fit one for the stage.'

'But she told me . . .'.

His expression grew thunderous. 'Oh, come on, Shan. I thought you'd have grown out of this persecution complex by now. Why can't you just admit you needed somewhere to make your film and Faraway was available and cheap.' As she opened her mouth to protest, he went on, 'I read about your search for a location, but I thought you'd know better than to come here and expect a welcome.'

Her senses reeled with the injustice of this. Not only had Tammy lied to her about King inviting her here, she had also lied to her father about the kind of training she'd been doing. How she had been able to keep her real career a secret from him, Shan couldn't guess. All she knew was that yet again Tammy had used her for her own ends.

'It seems there's been some kind of mis-understanding,' she said weakly. If only she hadn't been so tired she might have put up more of a fight but in her present exhausted state, she couldn't summon the energy.

'You're damned right there has. And it's just as well I got back early enough to do something about it.'

'What are you going to do?'

'It's not what I'm going to do—it's what you and your blasted crew are going to do. Pack up and be out of here first thing tomorrow.'

'I suppose there's no way I could get you to change your mind?'

'What do you expect?'

'Something I never got from you—understanding. But I suppose that was too much to ask.'

'Under the circumstances, yes. You were the one who left me for your producer-friend, remember?' At the same time, something unfathomable darkened his eyes. If she hadn't known better she would have said it was concern for her. He turned to leave.

She couldn't let him go, not like this. Suddenly she felt an urgent need to convince him that she wasn't as black as he was painting her. Since it was over between them she shouldn't care what he thought of her. She only knew that she did. 'Wait, please,' she implored. 'You're wrong about me leaving with Dave. I went to work with him, that's all.'

'I don't see what it has to do with me either way.'

'I don't either, I just want you to know the truth.'

He let his breath out in a ragged sigh. 'Truth? I don't know what the truth is where you're concerned. First there was your fantasy about Tammy trying to drive you away. Now this letter from me which has conveniently disappeared. You don't make it easy for me, do you?'

'At least on that score, we're even,' she shot back at him.

'You know, you're very beautiful when you're angry,' he said softly, startling her. His expression took on a yearning quality which tore at her heartstrings but she steeled herself against the sensation. What was the use when he always believed the worst of her?

'You win,' she said tiredly. 'We'll leave in the morning.'

At the weariness in her voice and manner, he relented a little. 'Look, I know I said first thing, but you don't have to leave as quickly as that. Take whatever time you need to pack and get organised.'

He sounded genuinely concerned. If anything, that was worse than his anger. 'Don't trouble yourself on my account,' she said stiffly, fighting an almost overwhelming urge to burst into tears. If he didn't go soon, she would break down completely. 'Doesn't Tammy need you or something?' she flung at him.

His face darkened. 'If she does, it's more than you ever did.' He left without another word and she slumped on to the bed feeling as if she'd just run the marathon. She should have known better than to come back here. It had all been too easy. Now, with the benefit of hindsight, she could see how Tammy had forged the letter to lure Shan's company here. Knowing that King objected to her becoming an actress, she had been hoping to complete her part in the film before he returned. If she hadn't had first hand experience of Tammy's duplicity, Shan wouldn't have believed anyone could be so underhanded.

Now, when she had finally learned to live without King, Tammy had forced her to go through the pain and humiliation of his rejection all over again.

The sight of him sitting in her room had awakened feelings she had tried to bury forever. The last three years had been kind to him, darkening his tan a little and deepening the two characteristic lines either side of his arrogant mouth. His eyes were a little more hooded and his neatly trimmed sideburns flecked with a fraction more grey, but it all added up to an even more formidable character than the one imprinted on her memory.

'You're beautiful,' he had said in that caressing way she had tried without success to forget. So he still thought so in spite of everything. She swallowed hard as her temperature began to climb. There was no point in thinking like that, no point at all.

But there was one thing she had to know. With a

longing glance at the now-vacant shower, she set off for the homestead. First things first.

Tammy was in her room when Shan knocked. 'Come in,' she trilled. Shan did as bidden, to find her stepdaughter clad only in a sheer black underslip, seated at her dressing table brushing her hair. Without turning round, she said, 'Leave the tea tray on the side table, Mrs G.'

'It isn't Mrs Gordon,' Shan said quietly.

Tammy spun around, her eyes wide with surprise. 'What are you doing here?'

Shan perched on the edge of the bed which was still covered with its little-girl floral coverlet. This room really should be redecorated in keeping with Tammy's present age, she thought irrelevantly, then remembered that it was no longer her concern. 'I came to see you. We have to talk.'

The teenager set her brush down on the dresser. 'Is it about my part? I was going to ask you whether you could give me more lines. I know I can handle them.'

'I'm sure you could. But there's no point because there isn't going to be a film now.'

Childish fury alternated with adult dismay in Tammy's expression. 'What do you mean, there won't be a film. I'm good enough, I know I am.'

'I didn't say you weren't.' Shan plucked awkwardly at the quilted coverlet. This was going to be much harder than she thought if the girl insisted on taking it so personally.

'Then if it isn't my acting, what is the problem?'

'King—your father—has ordered us to leave tomorrow. He doesn't want the film made here after all.' Her voice grew harder. 'But you knew that, didn't you, Tammy?'

Tammy thrust her full lower lip forward. 'If you know so much, why bother to ask me?'

Shan's head came up. 'I'm asking you because I want to know *why* you did it. You obviously expected King to be away a lot longer.'

'And he should have been!' Tammy's voice rose hysterically. 'I had it all figured out. He doesn't want me to be an acress like Mother, but it's all I've ever dreamed of being.'

'So while you were at school in Adelaide, you took drama lessons instead of your typing course, was that it?'

'Well he didn't care. He was too busy with his precious buffalo to check up on what I was doing.'

Shan rose to her feet in a fluid movement. 'He shouldn't have had to check up on you at your age. He trusted you.'

Tears began to cloud the teenager's luminous eyes. 'If he trusts me so much, why doesn't he trust me to make my own career decisions?'

Spreading her hands in defeat, Shan shrugged. 'I don't know. But I do know you did a wicked thing in forging his signature to that letter. You did take it from my luggage didn't you?' Tammy half-turned away, confirming Shan's guess. 'Well, it doesn't matter any more. We'll be going back to Sydney in the morning. I suppose losing the part will be punishment enough for you.'

Tears of rage and disappointment began to course down the younger girl's cheeks. Snatching up the hairbrush, she lunged at Shan. 'I hate you! I hate you! First you ruin my family life—now you've stolen my career as well!'

Before Shan could defend herself, the sharp bristles raked the side of her cheek and she felt the salt taste of blood at the corner of her mouth. Stunned, she stood rooted to the spot and brought a hand slowly up to her face then looked in amazement at the red stain on her fingers. 'Goodbye, Tammy,' she said and moved towards the door.

Tammy clutched at her arm. 'I'm sorry, Shan, please don't go yet. I didn't mean it.'

Ignoring the girl's pleas, Shan opened the bedroom door. Distantly, she heard a telephone ring and then King's clipped tones as he answered it. He sounded angry. But then he usually sounded that way when she was around.

'Shan, are you there?'

Instinctively, she retreated into Tammy's room but it was too late, King had seen her. 'Mrs Gordon said she thought you were here,' he said coldly. 'I want to talk to you.' His eyes widened as he noticed the scratches on her face and the traces of congealing blood. 'What's been going on here?'

'I was helping Shan do her hair and scratched her face by accident,' Tammy said at once, her expression defying Shan to contradict her.

'Is that true?' he asked, eyeing her suspiciously.

What did it matter? It was only a scratch. 'If Tammy says so.' She didn't feel up to arguing with either of them right now. 'What did you want me for?'

His steady gaze appraised her from head to foot and her pulses quickened as she thought of how he might once have answered that question. Then a shuttered look came over his eyes. 'I've just had a Mr Mortenson from the Bank of Sydney on the 'phone, wanting me to confirm that I'm your new backer.'

She felt the colour drain from her face. 'Oh no! I told him you weren't, but . . .'

His mouth tightened into a grim line. 'Another of your fantasies, Shan? I wonder where he got such an idea if not from you.'

Her shoulders slumped. 'I don't know. All I told him was that we were coming here to film. He arrived at the rest himself.'

His lips quirked upwards into a humourless smile. 'Very convenient, I'm sure.'

She couldn't take much more of this. 'It doesn't matter under the circumstances. I've told you we'll be leaving in the morning. I presume you told Mr Mortenson you had nothing to do with the film?'

'That and a few other choice things besides.'

Which was about what she'd expected. 'You'll be pleased to know you've just killed any chance I may have had of salvaging this project,' she told him.

'Surely funds aren't that hard to come by.' The look she gave him spoke volumes. 'I see. Well for what it's worth, I'm sorry if I had that effect. I was so annoyed at his presumptuousness that I reacted more strongly than I should have.'

'Oh, Dad, you've ruined my big chance.'

He turned on Tammy, his face set. 'Which reminds me, you have some explaining to do young woman. Is it true that you've been taking acting lessons behind my back?'

Tammy nodded dumbly, then an echo of her mother's spirit lit her even features. 'I had to audition and compete with a lot of other girls. Only two of us were accepted. I'm good, too—ask Shan.'

'Is she?'

'Yes. She has talent.'

King seemed to be fighting an internal battle with himself. After a few minutes' silence, he faced Shan. 'I want to talk to you in my study—alone.' The last was for Tammy's benefit and she subsided on to her bed, her expression chastened.

As she followed him out of the room, Shan wondered what on earth they could have to say to each other. He had made his position quite clear as well as ruining any chance she had of continuing the film into the bargain. Why couldn't he just let her leave quietly and be done with it? Did he need his pound of her flesh as well?

In his study, he gestured towards a leather covered armchair. 'Brandy and soda?'

So he remembered her favourite drink. 'Yes please.' While he mixed it she looked around, renewing her acquaintance with what had always been his favourite retreat. A battered old desk took up one corner. It was still piled high with reference books. A desktop computer had been added since she left, presumably to help him with the complex management of the property.

Around the walls were black and white enlargements of prize cattle and action shots of buffalo musters, wildlife and landscapes. He had always been keen on photography. Then her eye was riveted by a portrait hung in a shadowed corner, where she hadn't noticed it right away. It was a photo of herself, taken while she swam naked in the billabong, revelling in the unaccustomed freedom and the velvety feel of the water on her skin. She was surprised that he had kept it on display.

'You looked like a wood nymph,' he observed, following the direction of her gaze.

She coloured hotly, remembering what had come after the swim. They had lain on the bank, their bodies entwined like the roots of the pandanus palms around them. Only a mighty effort of will on King's part had prevented him from taking her at that moment.

It was obvious from the desire which blurred his eyes as he looked at her, that he remembered the moment too. 'You said you wanted to talk to me,' she said to cover her embarrassment.

He withdrew from the memory with an obvious effort. 'Yes. Is it true that you'll have to cancel the film if you can't get further funding?'

'There's no question of "if". The bank was my last hope.'

'And now I've ruined your chance with this Mortenson character?'

There was no point in denying it. 'I'm afraid so.'

He took a long pull of his drink then set the glass down then leaned against the desk with his arms folded. 'I'd like to make amends. Would you accept funding from me—on the usual business terms, of course?'

'Why would you do that?' she asked, bewildered. The answer was obvious, however. Now that he knew how much Tammy wanted a career in films, he would do anything to make it possible—even buy her a film if need be. 'I couldn't accept, of course, but . . .'

'But you'd accept a mutually beneficial proposition?' he queried, his eyes warming so that she had to look away lest he see the rush of response in her face.

'What could I possibly give you in return?'

'I fund the film and you continue where we left off before.'

Her head began to swim, whether with the brandy or the unexpectedness of his offer, she wasn't sure. 'You mean come back here, as your wife?'

'Exactly. I want you back, Shan, and if this is what it takes . . .'

'No!' she said wildly. 'That wasn't why I came back here.'

'But you are here, for whatever reason so the choice is yours. Stay here as my wife and your film can go ahead. Leave, and you haven't a prayer of finding another backer.'

Which sounded awfully like a threat, she thought shakily. With his influence in the business world, he could easily close off all avenues of funding to her. She thought of all the people who had worked so hard to make the project a reality. Their laughter as they relaxed outside after their demanding day reached her through the open window. Did she have the right to deny them the fruits of their labours when she could do something about it? 'I don't seem to have a choice, do I?' she said with a light-heartedness she didn't feel.

'Then I have your word that you'll stay?'

He knew she was cornered. 'Yes, I promise.' He hadn't set any time limits so even if she only endured the situation until the principle photography was finished, it would be worthwhile. Surely they could find the funds necessary for the post-production, once all the footage was in the can?

But was that the only reason she had agreed? a tiny voice inside her asked. Wasn't she clutching at this chance to make their relationship work, because deep down, it was the one thing she wanted more than any film?

He brought her down to earth with a crash. 'Now that I have your word, there's one more thing.'

Involuntarily, she tensed. 'Yes?'

'The new terms. There'll be no three-month trial this time. I want our marriage to be a real one in every sense of the word. My big mistake last time was in not putting my brand on you. This time, I intend to rectify that oversight. I'm not taking any chances on your straying again.'

He made her sound like one of his prize cattle, she thought wildly. She wasn't sure she was ready for a full relationship with him yet. There were too many unresolved issues. 'You didn't spell that out before you asked for my promise,' she said weakly.

His expression was unrelenting. 'You didn't ask.'

'All the same, you aren't fighting fair.'

'You know what they say about love and war, darling.'

She was tempted to ask him which this was, then decided against provoking him too much. He had already threatened to put his brand on her and she was afraid that in his present mood, he might have decided that now was as good a time as any.

He was watching her steadily. 'Is it a deal?'

He knew she regarded her word as sacred. She would never renege on a promise, no matter what was at stake. 'It's a deal,' she said and wondered what on earth she had let herself in for.

CHAPTER FOUR

SHE was still wondering when she stepped out of her long-delayed shower which was every bit as refreshing as she had hoped. She felt much more vital by the time she emerged from the bathroom swathed in a bath sheet, although she was still on tenterhooks thinking about the bargain she had made with King. If only he had allowed her some time to think! Catching her unprepared had been part of his plan, she was sure. But why? The most likely reason seemed to ensure that Shan stayed around long enough for Tammy to have her chance in the film.

She was so lost in thought that she almost cannoned into Rona, emerging from her room across the hallway. Dimly, she registered that Rona was rather overdressed for relaxing around the guest quarters. 'Where are you off to?' she asked curiously.

'Aren't you coming too?' queried Rona. Seeing Shan's look of confusion, she explained. 'Mrs Gordon has laid on a barbecue for us up at the big house.'

'I think I'll have dinner here and an early night,' Shan demurred.

Rona gave her a pitying look. 'The barbecue *is* dinner.' Shan hesitated and her friend gave her shoulder a playful shake. 'Come on! It will do you good to socialise for a bit. You know what they say about all work and no play?'

'I know. But I don't really feel like a party, honestly.'

Taking one look at her drawn expression, Rona propelled her into her own room and closed the door behind them. 'Now, tell Aunty Rona what's the matter. For a start, what happened to your face?'

Automatically, Shan touched a hand to the scratches on her cheek. 'I ran foul of a cat,' she explained, which wasn't too far from the truth.

'It wouldn't be a cat named Tamara, would it?' asked Rona shrewdly.

Shan regarded her friend with renewed respect. 'You should have been a mind-reader, you know.'

'I know. But right now, I'm too busy keeping an eye on a friend who shows every sign of terminal man trouble. Am I right?' Shan nodded slowly. 'Thought so. Your old nemesis, King Falconer, right?'

'Yes. Oh, Rona, he wants me to come back and live with him as his wife again.'

'Do you want to?

'No! That is . . . I don't know.'

'But he's made it a condition of allowing us to use Faraway.'

Shan nodded again. 'It seems he didn't want Tammy to take up acting but since she has and is good at it, he wants her to have her chance.'

Rona drifted to the dressing table and began rearranging the jars and brushes absently. 'So you're to be the sacrificial lamb.'

'Oh, it isn't as bad as that. He still cares for me, I'm sure.' It's just that he cares for his daughter more, she added to herself.

Rona whirled around. 'But what about what you feel? You've told me enough about your marriage so I know that he's anti-career. If you go back to him, won't that mean giving up everything you've built up? Are you sure one film is worth such a sacrifice? There are other films, you know.'

But not other men like King, her heart insisted. 'He didn't say anything about me giving up my work this time,' she said thoughtfully, 'but if I went back to him, I'd probably want to anyway.' She smiled self deprecatingly. 'You know me—All-or-Nothing Penrose!'

Rona's eyes widened in sudden understanding. 'And he's "all" isn't he? Because you're still in love with him.'

Quickly, Shan looked away. At once, Rona went to her and wrapped both arms around her. 'Go back to him then, if it's so important to you. As I said, there are other films—and other people to make them.'

The barbecue was in full swing by the time they joined the others. Shan had slipped into a brightly patterned pareo over her bikini, Rona having said that they would be able to swim in the homestead pool after the meal. She still didn't feel in a party mood but she had deciced to heed Rona's warning about all work and no play.

The barbecue area was as attractive as she remembered. The evening sun filtered prettily through a slatted pergola threaded with climbing plants, throwing attractive patterns of light and shade on to the cobblestoned courtyard. Perhaps two dozen people including film crew, cast and station hands were clustered around the courtyard. A few people were already enjoying the sparkling waters of the pool beyond the barbecue area. But she had eyes only for King.

He didn't seem to notice her at first, being too intent on tossing huge slabs of meat on to the massive bluestone barbecue. But as she hesitated on the fringe of the group, he passed the cooking tools to one of his stockmen and came striding over to her. 'I was beginning to think you weren't joining us.'

'It would have looked strange if I didn't,' she said through lips suddenly dry with apprehension.

'Is that the only reason you came?'

It wasn't and he knew it but she wasn't going to give him the satisfaction of admitting it. He had won his share of victories over her tonight. 'No, there was another reason,' she said, enjoying the gleam of satisfaction which sprang prematurely to his eyes. 'I was hungry.'

His expression became hooded and it was hard to tell whether he was angered by her flippant response or amused by it. 'I'll have to see what I can do about that appetite of yours,' he growled ambiguously.

A shudder of desire surged through her, catching her unawares. 'I don't know what you mean,' she dissembled.

He appraised her from head to foot with a raking stare which left her in no doubt that he was undressing her mentally. 'I think you do,' he said softly and went back to the barbecue, leaving her alone and curiously bereft.

She felt a strong urge to stamp her foot in frustration. He was impossible! While they were married he had treated her as some kind of vestal virgin although she had longed for the fulfilment of his possession. Now they were estranged, he turned every glance her way into an intimate encounter. It was as if their three years apart had banked fires of sexual desire in him which only she could extinguish. It was a disturbing idea, as she considered what his pent-up passion might be like once it was given release.

'Penny for them!'

Hot colour flooded her cheeks as she realised that Jason Cody was standing behind her, then she chided herself for her foolishness. It wasn't as if he could read her thoughts. 'Oh, hello,' she muttered.

'Try to contain your enthusiasm, darling. I know how much I mean to you.'

'Then you know better than to waste your time with me,' she rejoined.

He sighed dramatically. 'The chase is supposed to be half the fun, but I wish you'd tell me when we get to the other half.'

'I'll tell you if you ever do,' she said firmly.

He rolled his eyes upwards. 'You're a very difficult woman, Shan Penrose. I don't know why I persevere with you.'

'You can always give up,' she suggested, knowing it was futile. She caught sight of King watching them from his position at the barbecue. His expression was thunderous. Surely he wasn't jealous of Jason Cody? It certainly looked like it from the black looks he was directing at the two of them. If he hadn't been caught up with distributing the steaks while Mrs Gordon presided over the salad table, he would probably have intervened. A wicked idea occurred to her. Why not show him he wasn't the only one who could manipulate people's feelings?

She turned to Jason, bestowing on him one of her most dazzling smiles. 'I'm not all that hungry. Why don't you and I take a swim together, while we have the pool to ourselves. Everyone else is busy eating.'

A glint of enthusiasm lit his eyes. 'Since that is the most encouraging thing you've ever said to me, I'd better not say no. We can always eat afterwards.'

The suggestive way he said 'afterwards' made her wish she hadn't volunteered to swim with him. But she was committed now. Jason was already threading his way through the group towards the pool enclosure. She followed in his wake, aware without having to check, that King was watching every step of their joint progress.

As she felt his eyes on her, she was suddenly ashamed of her impulse to try to make him jealous.

Hadn't she condemned Tammy for her childish wish to 'get even'? Now here she was doing the same thing.

Her steps faltered but Jason grabbed her hand and pulled her towards the sparkling water. With a practised hand, he undid the tie of her pareo and the wraparound garment dropped away. He whistled appreciatively. 'With a figure like that, you should be in one of your own movies.'

She wished now that she hadn't worn such a revealing bikini, really only a few wisps of white jersey fabric held together with brass rings at the sides. When she put it on she hadn't been sure she would go into the pool, or if she did, had intended to be part of a crowd. 'I thought we came here to swim,' she said nervously as he continued to eye her.

Deftly, Jason stepped out of his shorts and swung his knitted shirt off over his head so he was revealed in figure-hugging navy trunks. His rigorous workouts in the gym and solarium showed in the athletic lines and trim, muscular build of his stock-in-trade—his Adonis-like body. 'Ready when you are,' he called and dived cleanly into the water.

Limp with relief, she followed more sedately, glad that at water level, a screen of brush box fencing hid them from the rest of the party. However, Jason behaved impeccably, stroking up and down the length of the pool with grim concentration. She watched him uncertainly for a few minutes then turned over on to her back and floated in the balmy waters. The wavelets lapped into her ears, shutting out the party sounds and enveloping her in a cocoon of peace.

Her tranquillity was shattered a moment later when Jason came up underneath her, trapping her in his arms. 'Put me down!' she spluttered as chlorinated water invaded her mouth and eyes.

'Not so loud, they'll hear you,' he admonished. 'I

didn't mean to choke you with water. Here, let me give you the kiss of life.'

She tried to struggle but was held fast against his muscular chest as he kissed her with rising passion. While he restrained her with one powerful arm, his free hand slid inside the skimpy band of her bikini briefs and she gasped with shock.

'No, please,' she begged in the brief interval when he released her mouth to take a breath.

'Let the lady go,' said a deadly calm voice from the poolside. 'You can see she doesn't appreciate your advances.'

Jason's head came up with a jerk. 'Stay out of this, it's none of your business.'

'Shan is my wife. That makes it my business.'

Panic gave her the strength to kick out violently, loosening Jason's grip on her body. While he was momentarily off balance, she struck out for the edge of the pool and hauled herself up on the side, where she sat shaking.

King eyed her with cold concern. 'Are you all right?'

'Yes, I'm fine thank you.'

In disgust, Jason swam to the far end of the pool and climbed out then padded away, dripping water. Minutes later they could hear his distinctive voice followed by a burst of laughter from the others.

She shot King a look of defeat. 'Now it will be all over the company.'

He shrugged. 'They had to find out sometime. I'm sorry if being married is going to cramp your style with your film star friend.'

'There's nothing going on between Jason and me, so you won't be cramping my style as you so crudely put it.'

His frown deepened. 'That wasn't how it looked

from where I was standing. Oh hell, Shan. This wasn't how I wanted things to be between us.' He reached for her hands and urged her to her feet on the tiled coping. Her damp skin came up against his firm body. Gently, he lifted a finger and stroked the scratches on her cheek. 'You should be more careful you know.'

Of accidents or Jason? she wondered, not sure how to take the caution. Her skin quivered where it was in contact with him and instinctively, she pressed herself closer.

With a groan, he pulled her hard against him so she felt the stirring of his need for her. 'Shan, Shan, you don't know what you're doing to me.' His fingers played up and down her bare spine with the skill of a pianist striking all the right chords, making her whole being vibrate with desire for him. Then his lips found the fleshy part of her earlobe and he nibbled on it sending waves of pleasure through her.

Unable to restrain herself any longer, she turned her head so that her mouth collided with his and she fastened on to it greedily, kissing him with an abandonment she hadn't believed she was capable of. 'Oh God, it's been so long,' she whispered.

'Too long,' he murmured back, his mouth moving against hers. 'Stay with me tonight.'

Wasn't this what she had wanted all along? To be truly his wife at long last? A high bell-like laugh reached her ears from the party beyond the brush box fence and she tensed, recognising Tammy's voice. It was a timely warning. If she gave in now, she would be at the mercy of Tammy's scheming with no hope of escape. 'No, I ... I need more time,' she said, wrenching herself away from his embrace.

He drew a long, shuddering breath. 'I suppose I will have to grant you that much. But I warn you, I won't wait forever. This time, I plan to make you my wife in every sense. Last time, I didn't brand you and I lost you. It's going to be different this time.'

Defensively, she wrapped her arms around herself. 'Do you have to talk about it as branding? You make me feel like one of your cattle.'

'I am a cattle man. I think in those terms. And what is lovemaking if not a man putting his mark of possession on a woman?'

Mark of possession—it sounded so final, so inescapable. She shivered again as he came forward but it was only to pluck a robe off a wall hook and drape it around her shoulders. She snuggled into the garment. 'Thank you.'

His expression was unreadable. 'Don't thank me for anything yet. You won't let me give you what I want to yet—but make no mistake, you will.' He laughed softly, mercilessly. 'There's always tomorrow.'

That night as she lay in her narrow bed in the guest quarters, it was tempting to wish tomorrow would never come. It was much easier to lie in the darkness, listening to the distant drone of a didgeridoo accompanied by the clack of music sticks and snatches of aboriginal song which drifted up from the billabong. The sound was comfortingly familiar, reminding her of all the other times she had listened to it when Faraway was her home. Now, however, she was in limbo, neither belonging here nor free to leave. With this disturbing thought in mind, it was a long time before she fell into a troubled sleep.

Fortunately next morning she had no time to indulge in self-pity. There was too much to be done organising the day's filming which was to take place at a billabong in the jungle some miles from the homestead.

So far the fact of her marriage to King had passed

unremarked so either Jason hadn't told them yet or
they had decided it was her business. Whichever it
was, she was relieved when no one stared or
commented.

After breakfast they were loading up the four-
wheel-drive convoy when King surprised her by
assigning one of his own stockmen to the group. 'I
hadn't budgeted for any extra crew,' she said
anxiously.

'Don't worry, he's on the Faraway payroll. I want
an experienced man with you in case you run into
problems with buffaloes or crocodiles.'

Was he concerned for her safety, or worried about
possible insurance claims? she wondered then decided
the thought was unworthy. 'That's very thoughtful of
you,' she told him. As she watched him ride away
from them she wished he had decided to come with
them himself. Which was a foolish notion. He had far
too much to do running the property.

As they negotiated the rough track through the
bush, she diverted her thoughts by counting the
anthills which towered like miniature Gothic cath-
edrals in the surrounding scrub. Taller than a man,
they were all aligned along the same north-south axis,
giving them an eerie precision. There was no sign of
the ants themselves but Shan knew they were there in
their millions. She had heard that they could eat the
inside out of a billiard ball.

'This is the place,' Dave Cameron called from the
lead vehicle. The convoy halted and they all piled out
to look around in awe at the sheer beauty of the
location.

King had suggested this place and it was as if he had
read Shan's thoughs, so exactly did it fit her mental
picture. Immense bamboos clustered around the edges
of the lagoon and mango trees trailed long festoons of

flowering creepers from their topmost branches. Bright fields of flowering lilies covered the lake margins and between them, slender, elegant ibis picked their way, lifting one delicate webbed foot after another, their needle pointed beaks poised to dart in among the roots for a frog or a brightly striped fish.

Birds flew in such numbers over the pool that it was as if they were contained in an invisible aviary. As well as the wading birds there were clumsy pelicans crash-landing in the centre of the lagoon, and in the trees, rosellas, and lurid cockatoos kept up a raucous chatter.

On the drive here they had glimpsed the lean ginger bodies and pert triangular ears of dingos but the wild dogs slid away into the scrub as they approached. Now as the noise of their engines died away, curious wallabies emerged from the spinifex and sat watching them from a safe distance.

'We should get some marvellous wildlife footage from here,' Dave observed, his eyes alight with enthusiasm.

It was a pity they had to work at all, she thought dreamily. This was a place to sit quietly, absorbing the beauty and feeling the presence of the unseen animals which she knew were all around them. With an effort, she shook off the indolent thought. 'Let's get to work.'

The surroundings seemed to infect everyone with a sense of lethargy. Moving was very nearly too much trouble in the oppressive humidity. But gradually, by a sheer effort of will, they captured on film an important scene where the young girl, Libby, was living wild with her aboriginal lover, both hiding from the wrath of their families.

Once or twice, Shan noticed Dave coaching Tammy in her part. He was spending a lot of time with her lately, she realised. Was this the start of a romance? Maybe it was just what Tammy needed. At least there was no chance that Dave would become another victim of the teenager's scheming. He had dealt with too many temperamental starlets in his career, not to be aware of any attempt to manipulate him.

By the middle of the day it was too hot to continue working so they broke for lunch and sprawled lazily under the paperbark trees.

'This is the life,' purred Rona as she handed Shan her packed lunch. The containers of chicken and salad had been prepared by the unit's cooks at the homestead and carried in insulated boxes in one of the vehicles. There were also cans of Coke and beer for those who preferred it. 'It's a darned shame we can't swim, though.'

Although the water looked tranquil and inviting, King had warned them that crocodiles lurked in the murky depths. The stockman had confirmed sighting several as he patrolled the banks while they were busy filming. Shan stretched luxuriantly. 'Swimming is too much trouble anyway. All I need now is a book of verse, a jug of wine and . . .'

'. . . and here comes "thou" to keep you company in the wilderness,' Rona finished for her.

Shan jerked upright as King rode into the camp. At the sight of his commanding figure astride one of his muscular station brumbies, her heart began to thud alarmingly. When he reached her, he slid easily from the saddle and dropped the reins over the horse's head so it would graze without straying. 'G'day,' he said laconically.

'Hello, King.' Why did he make her feel as gauche as a schoolgirl when he looked at her like that? 'I didn't expect to see you here.'

'I was rounding up some stray cattle not far from here so I thought I'd see how you were doing. You don't mind, I hope?'

'No, of course not.' Oddly enough, she didn't. Quite the opposite in fact. She found herself wishing the others a thousand miles away so she could be alone with him in this garden of Eden.

Rona scrambled to her feet. 'I'd better make sure that everyone has had enough lunch,' she said and scurried away.

'That was considerate of her.' He dropped to the ground, took a chicken drumstick from the box Shan proffered, and began to munch on it, the sunlight gleaming on his even white teeth. When he had finished he tossed the bleached bone into the water. 'Like this place?'

'It's beautiful,' she said unhesitatingly. 'Does it have a name?'

'It does now. Shan's Lagoon.'

She coloured with embarrassment. 'You can't call it that.'

'Why not? I can do anything I like with my property.'

The way he looked at her made her feel he was referring to more than naming a lagoon. 'Provided you can prove ownership,' she said warily.

He eyed her steadily. 'Oh I can prove it all right. You know what they say about possession and the law?'

Why did it always have to be possession with him? He wanted to possess her, to brand her—anything but to love her! Maybe that was an honour he reserved for his daughter. She got to her feet. 'I have to get back to work.'

'I had a horse once who kept running away,' he said quietly but in such a compelling tone that she froze in mid-step. 'I broke her in the end.'

Her steps quickened but his sardonic laugh followed her. As he mounted and rode off again, she remembered all too well seeing him break the wild station brumbies at the homestead. Usually, the job was done by a team of itinerant horse-breakers—black, brown and white—who worked their way around the countryside. But now and again King took a fancy to a certain horse and did the job himself.

She thought she knew which horse he was referring to. It was a handsome grey, taller than most brumbies and in surprisingly good condition. The first time he had tried to ride her, she had reared back and sent him flying like a rag doll through the dust then smashed a flailing hoof into his back. Shan's heart had been in her mouth as she watched but King had staggered back to the crush, mounting the grey again and again until she finally realised who was the boss.

Was that what he meant to do with her? Well he was in for a shock if he thought that. She was no brumby and it would take more than brute force to break her.

'For goodness sake, Shan, they're doing their best,' Dave said to her that afternoon, after she'd hauled the actors over the coals for a minor lapse in concentration.

'I only want to get this right, for all our sakes,' she snapped back.

He lifted an eyebrow. 'For our sakes, or to show the boss-cocky what an ace producer you are?'

'What's that supposed to mean?'

'You've been throwing your weight around ever since he rode in here at lunchtime. That isn't like you, Shan.'

She passed a hand over her eyes, acknowledging to herself that her behaviour had been a reaction to King's comments. 'I guess it's the heat getting to me.'

'Maybe we'd better call it a wrap then. We're ahead of schedule so we can afford an early finish for once.'

She was only too happy to concur. With everyone

helping, they were soon back on the road to the homestead, breathing a collective sigh of relief when it came in sight. There was a chorus of—

'Cold drinks.'

'A cool shower.'

'A dip in the pool.'

Mentally she agreed with these sentiments, but she arrived at her room in the guest quarters to find it bare of all her possessions. There was a note taped to the mirror which said simply, 'Your things are up at the house, King.'

He was nowhere in sight when she stormed into the homestead intending to protest at his high handed treatment but she was met by a concerned-looking Mrs Gordon. 'I know you preferred the other room but Mr Falconer insisted that I was to bring your things into here,' she apologised.

Some of Shan's anger evaporated. 'It's all right, it wasn't your fault.' She revised her plan to shift her things back, not wanting to get the kindly housekeeper into trouble.

'Mr Cody is still in your old room, so you're to have Mrs Falconer's room—that is, the one Joanna Price used to have,' Mrs Gordon amended.

Outside the bedroom door they almost collided with Tammy coming from the other direction. 'What are you doing here?' she asked ungraciously.

'It seems I'm moving in here.'

'Why are you going in there?' Tammy asked shrilly, as Mrs Gordon opened the door of her mother's old room. 'She can't have that room, I won't let her.'

'Now, now, Miss Tammy. Your father wants her in here and that's that,' the housekeeper soothed.

Tammy turned and stalked away but not before Shan caught a glimpse of such savage fury in her young face, that she was shaken. She followed Mrs

Gordon into the room and her eye went at once to a connecting door. 'Where does that lead?' she asked, trying to dismiss the threat she had read in Tammy's expression.

'That's Mr Falconer's room. He's still out with the men.'

As soon as Mrs Gordon left, she tried the handle of the door. It opened easily and there was no sign of a key. Beyond was King's unmistakably masculine room and her eye lingered on the big bed with its brown cord cover. Would he take her there, or come to her at night as she lay in the double bed in the room behind her?

As her temperature started to rise and her skin flooded with colour, she closed the door quickly. Surely she couldn't still want him after the way he had treated her? The ache in her loins answered the question for her.

There were no signs of her room's former occupant, although she guessed that the flamboyant pink and gold colour scheme had been Joanna's choice. The adjoining bathroom had a distinctly Hollywood character with its vast round sunken tub, gold plated fittings and thick white fitted carpet. She could well imagine the actress spending self-indulgent hours here.

A childish sense of excitement invaded her. She simply had to try out that marvellous bath. Since Faraway possessed an excellent spring-fed water supply she had no conscience about using so much water and soon filled the tub to capacity, adding a sprinkling of foaming bath crystals she found in a wall cabinet.

The water lapped around her breasts, the foam caressing her skin as she rested her head against the tiled surround. To think she had resisted such luxury!

Then she remembered that the comfortable suite had a price and she shivered in spite of the warm water enveloping her.

'My little wood nymph,' said a voice from the door. She started as King leaned over her, his eyes devouring the golden mounds of her breasts with their frosting of bath foam. Instinctively, she slid deeper into the tub, earning a mocking glance.

'I thought you were still out,' she said tensely.

'You mean you hoped I was. I told you, you can't run away from me forever.'

'I'm not running anywhere. I'm taking a bath.'

'Exactly what I had in mind after a hard day in the saddle.' To her dismay, he began to strip off his working clothes, dropping them in a heap at the side of the bath.

'What are you doing?' she demanded although she was afraid she already knew the answer.

'What does it look like? Taking a bath. That tub was built for two, after all.'

Before she could react, he stripped off his underpants and she had a brief glimpse of firm tanned flesh then he slid into the bath beside her.

As their thighs touched in the velvety water, she moved further away but he followed her and pulled her to him. The rough hair of his chest was slick with foam and she had no option but to cling to him or slip under the water. 'My God, you're lovely,' he breathed.

'Please, I need more time, King,' she begged, her eyes wide with appeal.

'Don't worry, I shan't rush you,' he assured her. To her astonishment, he began to bathe her with a crinkly sponge mitten which he scooped up from the side of the bath. It was an unbelievably sensuous feeling. Inside the mitt, his hand slid over her wet body, gently

but firmly massaging the bath foam into her skin. He
kept his eyes on her the whole time until she wanted to
scream for him to take her now because she couldn't
stand any more of this deliciously cruel tension.

'Please, King,' she mouthed, not sure how to put
into words what she wanted.

'That's more like it,' he mocked gently. 'But not yet.
It's my turn now.'

He slid the bath mitt over her unresisting hand and
lay back in the water with his eyes closed. She sat still
for a moment, not sure what she should do next. Then
diffidently she began to stroke the sponge down the
length of his body. 'Bit harder,' he murmured.

She felt like throwing the sponge at him. What did
he think she was, some sort of slave girl? Her thighs
ached with the need of him and she was supposed to
bathe him as if nothing was amiss. Then her hand
encountered his lean hardness under the water and she
realised that he was postponing his own pleasure as
much as hers, so that it would be infinitely more
rewarding when they finally succumbed.

Emboldened by the discovery, she passed the
sponge over his chest, gradually venturing lower until
she had massaged him all over with the mitt. Slowly,
he opened his eyes and rolled over in the water, taking
her into his arms so their bodies were entwined.

'Come here, wife,' he ordered.

She had a brief vision of the grey brumby coming to
him docilely after he had remounted it for the dozenth
time, and was tempted to spring out of the bath. But
her body betrayed her. She was aroused to such a
fever pitch that she could no more have left him of her
own accord than she could have flown.

As his mouth came crushingly down on hers she
surrendered completely to the heady sensations
transmitted down the full length of her body. No

matter what he had done to her, she was his and always would be. She was his wife in name and soon would be in every way. Even Tammy couldn't take that from her.

But as his hands moved possessively over her in the water, sending waves of pleasure surging through her, there was a knock on the bathroom door. 'What is it?' he said irritably, his voice hoarse with desire.

'You'd better come quickly, Mr Falconer,' came Mrs Gordon's terrified voice through the timber. 'It's Miss Tammy.'

CHAPTER FIVE

LIKE some kind of sea god rising out of the water, King stood up in the bath letting the droplets cascade off his magnificent body. 'God knows what she's done this time,' he said, his mind now totally focused on Tammy.

'Mrs Gordon didn't say what was wrong,' Shan said defensively. 'It may be a false alarm.'

He looked down at her, his expression scathing. 'On the other hand . . .'

In a swift, decisive motion he wrapped one of the bath sheets around his hips before opening the bathroom door. Mrs Gordon stood there, white-faced, too distraught to notice Shan still submerged in the bath. 'Now, what's going on?' he asked matter-of-factly.

His deliberately calming tone seemed to have an effect. Mrs Gordon swallowed convulsively. 'Tammy's locked herself in her room with . . . with my sleeping medicine. Oh God, Mr Falconer, what if . . .'

'That's enough!' he commanded sharply. 'You know what the doctor said. It may be just a bid for attention. She may not be planning anything at all. But I'll come and find out.'

Shan started to stir. 'I'll come too.'

'No, stay there. I've had more practice at this.'

For the first time, Mrs Gordon noticed her but was too distressed to be embarrassed. 'You'd better not, Shan. All this fuss is because you're sleeping in her mother's old room. If you come now it could make things worse.'

'She's right,' King added thoughtfully. 'I didn't

realise how she would take your moving in here. I thought she was over all that by now.'

To Shan, it was like being trapped in a recurring nightmare. 'I told you she won't be happy until I'm out of your life for good,' she said, her voice rising hysterically.

'That's a hell of a thing to say,' he snapped. 'You can't be so selfish that you'd want me to ignore my daughter when she needs me.'

Frustration and bitterness made her shrewish. 'For God's sake, go to her then! If she's more important to you than I am.'

What had possessed her to say such a vile thing? she asked herself in anguish after he and Mrs Gordon had gone. She lay for a few minutes longer in the rapidly cooling water then jumped up and dried herself roughly with a towel, swathing it around herself as she wandered into the luxurious bedroom.

She had little sympathy or concern for Tammy. Shan had seen the light of ambition in the teenager's eyes. There was no way she was going to take her own life when the success she dreamed of was within her grasp. But King couldn't see that. He only knew that he was being forced to choose between the two people he loved.

Shan had packed up and left rather than put him in that position before. Was history about to repeat itself?

She was still brooding on the possibility some time later when there was a knock on the door. She tensed then relaxed as she realised that if it was King, he probably wouldn't bother to knock. 'Come in,' she called.

Mrs Gordon entered carrying a tea tray. 'I thought you'd like your tea in here, Shan. After all the drama, nobody else feels like sitting down to a meal.'

'How is Tammy?' Shan asked dutifully. She felt she already knew the answer.

Mrs Gordon beamed. 'She's fine, thankfully. All that business with the sleeping draught was just an act to get attention, as Mr Falconer suspected. She had some crazy notion that you were trying to replace her mother but Mr Falconer assured her nobody would ever do that.'

Shan's head came up. 'He actually said that?'

'Well of course. He didn't mean he would never marry again—I mean, he married you, after all.'

'It's all right, Mrs G. I know what you meant.' Shan sighed. She was beginning to get the picture. The trial marriage had obscured King's real reason for marrying her, which was because he needed a woman in his life to satisfy his needs as a man. His precious conscience—to say nothing of his daughter's tender sensibilities—would never let him seek his pleasures outside marriage. But no woman would be allowed to take Joanna Price's place.

Why hadn't she seen it before? It wasn't Tammy she was competing with—at least, not directly. It was Joanna Price's memory. As long as Tammy forced King to keep Joanna enshrined in his heart, there was no chance for any other woman to win his love. The discovery was heartening in a way. At least it meant that Tammy's vendetta was not directed at her as a person, but would have been directed at anyone who threatened to replace Joanna in her father's life.

The knowledge cheered her sufficiently to entice her to sample the tea Mrs Gordon had prepared. On the tray was a ham and tomato omelette with a crisp side salad and a bowl of fresh strawberries. She made a tentative start on the omelette and discovered that she had quite an appetite. Finishing it off, she reached for the strawberries and was half-way through the bowlful when there was another knock on the door.

It was probably Mrs Gordon returning to collect the tray. 'Come in, Mrs G.,' she called warmly.

'I'm glad to see your temper has improved,' King said as he walked in.

'I thought you were Mrs Gordon,' she said, flustered.

His eyes narrowed. 'I should have known that welcoming tone wasn't for me.'

It could have been if only he would give her a chance. 'About this afternoon,' she ventured, 'I'm sorry for the things I said.'

'Apology accepted, we were all on edge.' He placed a bottle of brandy and two glasses on her tray. 'I thought you might have a drink with me . . . since we were so rudely interrupted before.'

So he thought they would just take up where they left off. 'I'd like the drink,' she agreed, 'would you leave it for me, though? I'm rather tired and was about to go to bed.'

'So was I,' he said, his tone becoming warm.

'That wasn't what I meant,' she said hastily.

He came up behind her and began to massage her shoulders with firm strokes. 'You were willing enough earlier.'

'But that was before . . .' She clamped her mouth shut, her eyes widening. She hadn't meant to say that.

His hands dropped to his sides. 'Before Tammy needed me,' he finished for her. 'So you're still blaming me for going to her, aren't you.'

'You did what you thought was right.'

'But you don't happen to agree.' He went over to the window and stood gazing out, his arms folded and his shoulders hunched.

She resisted the urge to go to him and wrap her

arms around his shoulders which spoke so eloquently of his internal struggle. 'Whether I agree or not is irrelevant. It happened and neither of us can change it.'

'So where do we go from here?'

She poured some of the brandy into the two glasses and held one out to him. He took it and their fingers brushed for a mere second but it was enough to send sparks of electricity shooting up her arm. She pulled back with a jerk, spilling some of the brandy. As he blotted it, she said, head downcast, 'I don't think there's anywhere for us to go.'

His eyes clouded. 'So I am being punished for going to Tammy instead of staying with you.'

'It's not like that at all,' she protested.

He downed the drink in one swallow and set the glass down on the window ledge. 'Isn't it? You've been competing with her from the day you two met. Can't you see that I love you both equally, but in different ways?'

'It's Tammy who can't see it!' she cried, unable to restrain herself any longer. 'She doesn't want you to love me, King. She doesn't want you to love anybody except Joanna.'

She knew she had said too much when she saw his face darken like the threat of an approaching storm. 'You just can't leave that poor child alone, can you? She wants me to be happy, even if it means I marry again—she's told me so herself. What do you want me to do? Ask her to leave Faraway?'

Yes! her mind screamed but she knew it would be the last straw if she said so. 'Do what you like,' she said bleakly. 'You usually do anyway.'

He disappeared through the connecting door, slamming it violently behind him so that the wood reverberated with the shock. Unhappily, she listened to sounds of him getting ready for bed. They were more distinct than usual as he vented his anger on anything handy.

Why couldn't he see that she was right? No matter what Tammy told him, she blamed Shan for the break-up of her parents' marriage and wouldn't be happy until she had driven Shan out of her father's life. In a way, Shan even felt sorry for the teenager. Her plan to lure the film company here had backfired when King returned earlier than expected. Now she couldn't enjoy her new career because of her bitterness over Shan's reunion with King.

From next door came the soft thud of clothes being dropped one by one on to the floor, then came the creak of the mattress as he eased his weight on to it. She knew that he slept naked, having talked about sleepwear with him once only to be told that he didn't wear any, so it was easy to visualise his husky brown shape with only a sheet for covering. Her pulses quickened and she licked her lips restively. She couldn't go on like this for much longer, tortured by what Tammy was determined she would never have.

What if she tried to talk to her stepdaughter, reason with her? Surely at eighteen she should be able to see the illogicality of her behaviour, as well as the ultimate cruelty when she married one day and left her father alone? She might refuse to listen but Shan felt compelled to make the attempt. What else could she do, short of consigning her marriage to the scrap-heap?

Next day, however, she had no chance to talk to Tammy because the teenager wasn't listed on the call sheet. This meant she was not needed for the scenes being filmed that day. Telling herself they could still have their talk at the homestead at the end of the day, Shan made an effort to concentrate on her work.

The scene called for Jason Cody, as the station owner, Ben Drysdale, to try to find out from his stockmen, where the young aboriginal boy might be hiding with his daughter, played by Tammy.

Jason had been avoiding Shan since the disastrous encounter in the swimming pool when he had been humiliated by King. The actor was too much of a professional to let it affect his work, but off the set, he had been cold and cutting in the few words he'd exchanged with Shan. Once or twice she had seen him with his head bent close to Tammy's, talking about their parts, she assumed. However, it unnerved her that they fell silent as soon as she came within earshot.

Today's scenes were to be filmed against a background of the breaking-yard. The indoor scenes of the homestead would be constructed in a studio thousands of miles from here, in Sydney.

Some of the real stockmen had been roped in as extras, to add colour and authenticity to the scenes. Actor's Equity insisted, however, that all the actors with speaking parts were union members.

When the actor who was to play the stockman interviewed by Jason arrived, Dave directed him to his place along the breaking-yard fence. There was a wild brumby pacing around the yard, its nostrils flaring, and the actor eyed it nervously. 'It can't reach me up here, can it?' he asked.

'Buncha sissies,' jeered the real stockman. 'Course it can't reach you up there—just don't fall off the rail, that's all.'

The young actor took a firmer grip on the railing so that his knuckles whitened. 'It won't do,' objected Shan. 'You're supposed to look as if this is your second home. You take wild horses in your stride, remember?'

Still the actor couldn't relax and kept eyeing the

wild-eyed horse below him with distrust. 'Like this!'
Shan said impatiently, hopping up on to the fence.
She draped herself over the rails in the same careless
fashion she'd seen King adopt after a punishing ride
on a half broken horse.

'What the bloody hell is she doing up there?' came a
voice tight with outrage.

She was so startled that she almost lost her balance
and would have fallen into the yard under the
brumby's flailing hooves, if she hadn't been caught in
strong arms and lifted bodily down from the railing.

'Don't you have more sense than to take risks like
that?' he demanded furiously, his hands still encircling
her slender waist.

How dare he humiliate her in front of her own crew
like this? 'Take your hands off me,' she said icily. 'For
your information, I was merely demonstrating the
proper way to sit on that fence for the benefit of the
actor.'

'And you've had oh-so-much experience, haven't
you?' he said mockingly. 'Another second and you'd
have been under that horse's hooves.'

'Not if you hadn't startled me the way you did.'

At once, Dave Cameron moved placatingly between
them. 'Take it easy, Shan. I'm sure we're grateful that
Mr Falconer grabbed you when he did.'

'I'm not grateful for anything from *Mister* Falconer,'
she hissed back in a tone for his ears alone. 'Now
would you mind leaving? You're interfering with my
work.'

'You're forgetting that I do what I like with my
property,' he reminded her in a menacing voice, his
eyes fixed on her so she was in no doubt as to what he
meant.

She was about to retort that she wasn't his property
yet—and never would be if Tammy had her way,

when she remembered the actors and crew clustered around them, watching with intense interest. 'Can we finish this discussion later!' she appealed.

'Thanks for the invitation, I accept.' He tipped his broad-brimmed hat to her.

'It wasn't an invitation and you know it,' she hissed back. Then as one of the cameramen chuckled softly, she flared, 'Take it any way you like. Just get out of my way.'

'Actually, I was going to offer to coach your actors in breaking-yard etiquette,' he offered. 'But since you feel I'm in the way . . .'

'Not at all, Mr Falconer,' intervened Dave smoothly. She could have hit him. 'I think that's a great idea, don't you, Shan? It will make the scene so much more convincing.'

He had said the one thing calculated to make her weaken and he knew it. Damn Dave! He knew her too well. 'Oh, all right,' she capitulated. 'but only in the interests of a better film.' There, let him get satisfaction out of that if he could. From the way his mouth tightened into a grim line, she knew her comment had displeased him.

Nevertheless, watching the way he coached the actors, she had to agree that Dave was right. It would make a difference if the actors looked and behaved like bushmen instead of nervous city slickers.

To make things more realistic, he had some of his own men manhandle the defiant brumby into the crush—a narrow railed enclosure where it could be saddled ready for the breaker to mount it. The actors were clumsy in their attempts to get the saddle on to the rearing beast, but their confidence grew with each try until they at least looked as if they were accustomed to dealing with such situations.

When Shan announced that they would try for a take, the make-up people rushed in to blot some of the

grime off the actors' faces. 'Leave it,' ordered King.
'I've yet to see a bushman without sweat or dust or
both on his face.'

'Kindly leave the orders to me,' Shan snapped then
had to add sheepishly, 'but he's right, leave the men as
they are. They do look more convincing that way.'

The scene went well after that so they were able to
get it in only three takes. Some scenes took dozens of
attempts before a version was usable. Reluctantly,
Shan had to agree that King's intervention had made
things much easier. If only he was as helpful where
she was concerned!

When they broke for lunch, he came over to her.
'I'm sorry if I did the wrong thing earlier,' he said, not
sounding in the least contrite.

'I don't want my authority being undermined,' she
said quietly. 'I'm sure you of all people know how
important that is.'

He nodded thoughtfully, glancing around at his own
men, dotted among the film people. 'I hadn't thought
of it that way. It's as important for your orders to be
readily obeyed as it is for mine. Although in my case,
it's usually a matter of life and death.'

'It can be in this business, too,' she reminded him.
'Particularly if there's a stunt involved, or some
special effects like explosions called for.'

'I've already said I'm sorry,' he said edgily. 'What
more do you want?'

'Nothing. Nothing at all from you.'

'That's right, you made yourself quite clear on that
point last night, didn't you?'

'I tried to, but you're too stubborn to see anyone's
point of view but your own,' she flared up.

'So now I'm the one who's stubborn!'

'Look, I thought we were going to talk about this
some other time,' she said wearily.

'With you, some other time never comes,' he sneered and spun on his heel.

She was reluctant to let him leave on such a note. 'Where are you going?'

'I have some business to attend to in Katherine,' he snapped back. 'It's quite obvious that I'm not welcome around here.'

'If you'd only think about what I said last night, you'd see things differently,' she said despairingly.

He looked at her in disgust. 'You never let up, do you? Well if it makes you any happier, I *did* think about what you said—and got precious little sleep last night into the bargain.'

'But what did you decide?' she persisted, feeling her heart thud with apprehension. This was the nearest he had ever come to admitting that she might have a point.

'I didn't yet,' he said tersely and strode off towards his Land-Rover.

Watching him go, she felt her spirits lift a little. At least he hadn't dismissed her accusations out of hand as she had half-expected him to do. Surely if he gave the matter some more thought he would see that she was right. Tammy *was* trying to drive them apart because she didn't want any other woman to take Joanna's place in her father's life.

'He's really something, isn't he?'

She spun around as Rona came bearing down on her with their lunches which they'd developed the habit of eating together under the bougainvillaea. 'Yes, he is,' she confirmed wistfully.

'But it still isn't working between you two, huh?' She grinned. 'That scene this morning was very public, you know.'

Shan coloured. 'I know. But whenever we get within two feet of each other, we seem to strike sparks off one another.'

'Sounds like love to me,' Rona sniffed.

'Is that what you call it? I'd call it guerilla warfare.'

They ate their boxed lunches in silence for a while, enjoying the balmy day with the paintbox blue sky overhead like a canopy and the caterwauling of cockatoos as they moved in flocks from one tree to another. 'It's Tammy, isn't it?' Rona said breaking the silence between them.

'Is it so obvious?'

'It is to me. I've known you a long time, remember. All those midnight coffee sessions working on applications for the film commission were a great way to get to know somebody. Doesn't she like you?'

'It's more than that.' Haltingly, Shan explained her belief that Tammy didn't want anyone taking her mother's place. 'She idolised Joanna Price,' she finished.

'How well did she know her mother?'

Shan frowned. 'I'd say not very well. She obviously has no idea what other people thought of her.'

'You mean she doesn't know about the drinking?' Shan shook her head. 'Or the affairs with all her leading men? To say nothing of her fits of temperament and lapses of memory brought on by alcohol abuse.' She looked stunned. 'You mean Tammy doesn't know any of that? My God, she's eighteen years old and working in her mother's business. How could she not know?'

'King has kept most of it from her, only telling her the flattering parts, I gather. Remember, we didn't even know Joanna had a daughter, so she's been pretty sheltered,' Shan explained. 'He can't see that by putting Joanna on a pedestal, making her look like some sort of saint, he's given Tammy the idea that no other woman could possibly take her place.'

Rona crumpled their lunch wrappers into a tight ball.

'Sounds like *Mission Impossible* to me. Can't you tell her the truth about Joanna?'

Miserably, Shan plucked at a strand of grass and chewed on it. 'I couldn't. In the first place, she would never believe me. And in the second, King is afraid it would destroy her.'

'So you're going to let her push you out of your husband's life, ruining your own chance at happiness to protect her, is that it?'

'That's about it,' Shan said ducking her head so Rona wouldn't see the tears which blurred her eyes. 'Rona, I'm no saint, but there's no future for us the way things are.'

'And no future for you if you leave here.'

Her appetite suddenly gone, Shan pushed the last of her lunch away from her. 'You finish this, I'm not hungry any more.'

'All right, if you're sure?' She paused. 'By the way, someone left a note for you in the make-up van.'

'What about?'

Rona shrugged. 'Beats me. It's in a sealed envelope. Maybe a love note from a secret admirer.'

'Fat chance of that!' Still, Shan was curious as she made her way to the make-up van. Who would be leaving notes for her? She had her answer as soon as she saw the scrawling handwriting on the envelope. It was from King.

'Dear Shan, I've been thinking about your relationship with Tammy and I feel I owe it to you to at least discuss it if there's to be any chance for us. I'll be away at Katherine until late but if you wait for me on the verandah at ten tonight, we can talk there without disturbing the rest of the household. King.'

Her heart began to race. So he had given her

suggestion some thought after all, and had realised that she wasn't speaking out of jealousy but real concern for Tammy and their marriage.

Maybe there was a chance for them after all. She fought down her rising hopes. It was too early for such things yet. But perhaps after tonight, they could start again and have the sort of relationship she had dreamed of forging between them.

She got through the afternoon's filming somehow, although she was so distracted that once or twice, Dave had to call her attention back to the job on hand. Late in the day, Tammy drifted down to watch Jason Cody at work and she stared at Shan suspiciously when the other woman gave her a radiant smile.

Under Tammy's scrutiny, Jason was on his best behaviour as he always was when he sensed he was in the presence of a fan. And fan Tammy apparently was. She hung on the actor's every word, asking his advice on handling her own part, and flirting with him in a shameless way.

'Doesn't Cody know better than to carry on with a girl half his age?' Dave Cameron said sulkily.

'You know Jason. He loves to have admirers, especially female ones.'

'But I didn't think he went in for cradle snatching.'

Shan looked at Dave curiously. Was there more to his interest in Tammy than he was admitting? His attitude towards Jason certainly smacked of old-fashioned jealousy. Shan smiled to herself, earning Dave's displeasure.

'What's so funny? I was only thinking of Tammy.'

'I'm sure you were,' she agreed. Now that there was a chance she could straighten things out between her and King, she felt magnanimous, at peace with herself and the world.

It was only when she stopped to consider how she

felt that she realised she hadn't felt this *right* since they split up three years ago. It was as if part of herself had been missing and she was only now about to get it back.

In this lighthearted mood, she joined Tammy and Mrs Gordon for dinner in the family room. With King still away, Shan had agreed with Mrs Gordon's suggestion that they eat informally. The rest of the company had opted for a barbecue down by the billabong.

'They're enjoying their stay here,' Shan told Mrs Gordon.

The housekeeper looked pleased. 'We love having you here, don't we, Tammy.'

The teenager studiously avoided answering, giving her quiche-lorraine her full attention.

'Well I've loved having you here,' Mrs Gordon amended, adding wistfully, 'You don't have to go away again, do you, Shan?'

At this, Tammy's head came up and she fixed Shan with such a glare of hatred that Shan shivered. Did the girl know that she and King were on the verge of reconciling their differences? 'I don't know yet,' Shan said carefully. 'I hope King and I can work something out.'

'I do, too dear. I know it's all very modern to live apart and have your own lives, but I'm old-fashioned enough to believe that married couples should be together.'

With a sob, Tammy leapt up from the table and ran from the room. As Shan moved to follow her, Mrs Gordon restrained her. 'Let her go, dear. I put my foot in it by saying couples belong together, forgetting of course that her Mum and Dad didn't belong together at all. I've never seen a more relieved man than Mr Falconer when he got the final papers for the divorce. Dropped ten years off his age, he did.'

They finished the meal in subdued silence, although Shan couldn't entirely suppress her feeling of anticipation. Her eye kept shifting to the grandfather clock as the hands moved agonisingly around. To help pass the time, she insisted on clearing the table and helping Mrs Gordon with the washing up.

'But that's what we have a dishwasher for,' she protested.

'I know. But I like to feel useful.'

It was after nine o'clock by the time they finished tidying everything away, Shan having obtained several favourite recipes from Mrs Gordon. They would come in handy when she was cooking for King again, she thought happily then reminded herself that this thought was premature.

In her room, she changed out of the cotton sundress she'd been working in, and dressed in a silky halter-necked dress which had been one of King's favourites during their brief marriage. She made herself dawdle over brushing her hair to a glossy fullness which crackled with electricity in the dry air. Finally, she dabbed cologne on her fevered skin and glanced at the clock. It was two minutes to ten.

The rest of the household was in darkness as she slipped down the corridor towards the front verandah. The wide, shady structure ran the full length of the house and was so cool during the heat of summer that the family spent as much time there as indoors during the hottest days.

Her sandalled feet made no sound on the polished timber boards and at first, she thought she was alone on the verandah. Then she caught the red glow of a cigarette tip in the shadows. 'King?' she said uncertainly.

The figure stirred slightly in the shadows then the cigarette was extinguished and he held out his arms to her. With a little cry, she went into them. 'Oh, King!'

As soon as the strong arms enfolded her, she knew she had been duped. 'Jason!' she gasped, twisting in his iron grip. 'Let me go!'

'Not this time, Mrs Falconer,' he said nastily. 'You made a fool of me once, but you aren't getting away with it this time. Your gallant cattleman is still away, so there's nobody to come to your aid now.'

'But the note?' Her head was spinning.

'Your loving stepdaughter helped me with that. She does rather a good job of Daddy's signature, don't you think?'

So that was what Jason and Tammy had been conspiring about. She should have remembered how good Tammy was at forgery! 'All right, you've had your fun, now let me go,' she said as coldly and authoritively as she could.

His teeth gleamed in the shadows. 'I haven't had my fun yet, but I intend to.'

To her mortification, he tore at the tie fastening of her halter dress so it slipped down to her waist, exposing her full breasts which were innocent of any covering. 'Oh God!' she gasped. Her hands were still imprisoned so she couldn't even make a move to cover herself. 'Think, Jason!' she said urgently. 'If this gets out, you'll never work again in the industry.'

'But it won't get out,' he said smoothly. 'It would just be your word against mine—and I've a feeling you wouldn't want hubby to find out.'

Her mind was in turmoil, but even in her confusion she could see how hard this would be to explain to King. He had believed her the first time when she said there was nothing between her and Jason. A second time would be asking too much. 'You bastard!' she ground out, struggling in his grip.

His hold tightened. 'That's the girl! I like a bit of spirit in a woman.' Resist though she might, he urged her backwards until she was spreadeagled on the swing seat with Jason half-lying on top of her. Hungrily, he clamped his mouth on hers so she had no chance to scream for help. His weight and athlete-fit body made her no match for him. She was helpless and he knew it.

'What the hell! So this is what you get up to the minute my back is turned.'

As the verandah was flooded with light, Jason jerked upright and Shan looked past him to see King braced in the doorway, his hand still on the light switch. 'King, thank God!' she gasped. 'I thought you were still away.'

'Obviously,' he said in such a vicious tone that she shuddered. 'Get off her Cody before I kill you.'

Cowed by King's manner, Jason slunk off into the house like a whipped dog, not even glancing back towards Shan. 'You don't think this was my fault?' she asked tremulously.

King's eyes raked her from head to foot, his expression contemptuous. 'I find you half naked and rolling on a couch with that bastard. What the hell am I supposed to think?'

'Not what you're obviously thinking. I was lured out here by Jason so he could get his revenge for the way you humiliated him the other night.'

His face remained set and grim. 'Even if I accept your explanation, I can still see I've made a big mistake.'

'What do you mean?' she asked uncertainly, not liking the way he was looking at her.

'Without a brand, a member of the herd is always in danger of straying and being appropriated by someone else.'

'King, I wasn't straying as you put it. And I'm not a member of your herd—I'm your wife.'

'Not yet,' he said grimly. 'But you're going to be.'

She was too shocked to resist as he scooped her up in his muscular arms and carried her into the house.

CHAPTER SIX

'KING, don't, please—this is rape,' she pleaded as he carried her down the darkened corridor towards his room.

'Is it?' he asked tautly. 'I don't see you putting up much of a struggle.'

He was right. She should fight him, scream and try to kick her way free. He would have to release her to avoid waking the household. So why did she lie meekly in his arms and allow him to carry her to his bed?

Because, to her eternal sorrow, it was what she wanted. She had dreamed of this moment for so long, reading its promise into what she thought was his note.

'Admit it,' he said softly, caressingly, 'you want this as much as I do.'

'You're wrong,' she said without conviction. There was no way she was going to admit to him how much she loved him. That would be the ultimate humiliation. Knowing there was no future for them, it was better if she went away before he found out. At least this way, she still had her self-respect intact.

They reached his room and he placed her gently down on the vast bed which had been turned down to reveal cream coloured sheets edged in dark tan. Her dress was still open to the waist and the sheet felt cool against her back.

He stood over her, looking his fill at her creamy flesh, then reached out a hand and caressed the tumble of tawny hair which spilled across the pillow like a halo.

At his touch, a tremor shook her. 'Please, King . . .'

'Please, King—no, or please, King—yes?'

She wasn't even sure herself which one she meant by that tremulous phrase.

He made the decision for her, stripping off his clothes with economical movements and letting the garments fall where they may on the floor. Soon he stood before her, magnificent in his nakedness, and all her thoughts of resistance fled.

With a new assurance she held out her arms to him. With a groan, he snapped off the light and stretched full length on the bed beside her, burying his head between the soft mounds of her breasts.

If she couldn't have him for a lifetime, she could have this moment to remember, she decided distantly, her body already making the decision for her by stirring to vibrant life. He sensed her surrender and propped himself up on one elbow beside her. 'Do you usually come to bed half dressed?'

Her lower body was still clad in the halter necked dress, its straps trailing around her legs. She wriggled out of the skirt and kicked it off the end of the bed. 'Is that better?' she asked shyly.

His eye appraised the slim contours of her body and he murmured his appreciation, only pausing when he reached the lace bikini briefs which were her last covering. She allowed him to slide them down around her ankles, then she kicked them off too and snuggled close against him, her skin quivering with anticipation which crackled through her being like an electric charge.

Slowly, ever so slowly, he stroked a hand down the length of her body and a tremor shook her. 'Are you cold?' he asked in concern.

She smiled. 'If I get any warmer, I'll burst into flames.'

She was on fire with desire for him. It was like a bushfire, raging through her. But he continued to stoke the fires by caressing her with ever more possessive strokes, seeking out the most intimate recesses of her body to bring them to tingling life with his touch.

'Oh God, King,' she breathed when she could stand it no longer. 'It's yes, definitely, yes.'

Still he prolonged the sweet torment, although she could see that it was taxing his iron control to the limit. Just when she thought she must explode with the force of her pent-up desires, he claimed her with fierce and tender passion.

Their lovemaking was even more exhilarating than she had dreamed. Gently but inexorably he drove her upwards to heights of passion she had never known she could experience. When she thought they could go no higher, he took her to new pinnacles until she was dizzy with the tumultuous sensations raging within her. Finally the sensations blurred into one intense kaleidoscope of feeling.

Then it was over and she lay trembling beside him, drained of everything but an all-consuming love for him. She was shaken by the force of her own responses. He had acted on her system like a powerful drug, and she was afraid that having tasted it, she would hunger for it for the rest of her life.

At the same time her mood was tinged by an inescapable sadness. She had dreamed of becoming his wife, but not like this—not because he wanted to prevent her straying to another man by—how did he term it?—putting his brand on her. Well he had done that. She was his wife and even if they parted physically, only death could part them spiritually from now on.

'Hold me, King,' she whispered, needing the

comfort of his arms to drive away the coldness this thought brought with it.

He made no move towards her, seemingly content to let his eyes make love to her as she lay stippled by the moonlight which streamed in through the window. 'What is this? Look but don't touch?' she asked uncomfortably.

'Something like that. I've been waiting for this moment for so long that I'm having trouble believing you're actually here beside me.'

'I would have been here a long time ago if you hadn't insisted on the trial period,' she reminded him.

'I thought it was the way to make sure you would stay. But I was wrong. I should have made ours a real marriage right away.'

'But a marriage is more than just a physical relationship,' she protested. 'It wasn't enough to keep you and Joanna together.' She saw his face darken and turned her head away. 'Oh, King, I didn't mean that.'

His mouth tightened into a hard line. 'Yes, you did, and you were right. It wasn't enough for us. But it's different for you and I. You can't deny how you felt just now.'

There was no point in denying it. He had been as aware as she was of the effect he was having on her during those unguarded moments. 'I can't deny you satisfy me physically,' she said carefully. 'But it isn't enough to make a marriage work.'

His breath came out in a tense explosion. 'Then tell me what is, for God's sake.'

She hadn't wanted to have this discussion now, but since he insisted it might as well be said. 'I want what Shakespeare called "a marriage of true minds". That means being a team. As long as we're divided . . .'

'Divided over Tammy—why don't you say it?'

Her eyes flashed fire. 'All right, I will. We are

divided over Tammy because she's done everything she can to keep us that way.'

'Look I admit she can be trying but she's had a rough time what with the divorce, and Joanna's death.'

'I keep telling myself that, but I've about run out of excuses for her. As long as she believes that her mother was some sort of goddess, she will never accept a mere mortal like me in her place.'

'That's absurd.'

'Is it? Does she know the reasons why you divorced Joanna? Her drinking, her affairs and other problems? I'm sorry if this hurts you, King, but it needs to be said.'

His face contorted. 'How can I tell her such things about her mother? It would destroy her.'

'She's more resilient than you think, and she's entitled to know the truth. It might make her mother's desertion easier for her to live with. At the moment it looks to me as if she's searching for reasons to explain it to herself. She even tried to blame me for coming between you and Joanna.'

He raked a hand through his hair. 'I can soon straighten her out about that. But I can't risk her mental stability by telling her the rest.'

'Can't or won't? Isn't it that you won't tell her what Joanna was really like because it would mean admitting that you made a mistake—and the Cattle King never makes a mistake.'

'You sure know how to wound with words, don't you?'

'I should. I've been a victim of them often enough myself. But I suppose it doesn't make much difference now.'

He regarded her suspiciously. 'What are you trying to say?'

'I'm saying that I still can't stay here. There's no future for us as long as Tammy keeps thrusting Joanna's memory between us.'

He got up and went to the window where he stood profiled against the moonlit sky, his form even more breathtaking in silhouette. 'I don't think you have the option of walking away any more. You're forgetting that you're my wife now—in every way.'

How could she forget? Her body was still throbbing with the memory. I hadn't forgotten how hard it is for you to give up a possession, if that's what you mean. But you can't force me to stay even so.'

He looked at her in mild surprise. 'I don't think force will be necessary. You need me as much as I need you. Don't deny it, you gave yourself away in bed.'

Oh God, had she betrayed herself as thoroughly as that? 'You're confusing the heat of passion with something else,' she protested.

'I'm not the one who's confused,' he assured her. 'You may not be aware of it yourself yet, although I doubt it, but I give you something you need desperately—completeness. You've tasted it once, my darling, and now you'll crave it forever. I'm an addiction.'

It was so exactly how she had felt while he was making love to her that her determination faltered. It was as if he had invaded her mind as well as her body. She felt the need to repel him quickly, while she still had an identity left. 'Addictions can be satisfied in other ways,' she said defiantly.

He paled and his jaw worked before he answered. 'You mean Jason?' Her expression of revulsion answered for her. 'Then it must be Cameron,' he hazarded. 'Of course! You ran away from me once before to be with him.'

'Not to be with him, to work with him, there's a difference,' she corrected tiredly. 'But it's not Dave Cameron in any case. There's nobody—yet,' she added provocatively.

'You little . . .' He started towards her. In a panic, she leapt from the bed and darted through the connecting door to her own room, propping a chair against the door to stop him from opening it.

She waited tensely beside the door for a few minutes but he made no attempt to follow her so she climbed into her bed which felt cold and unwelcoming against her bare skin. It was too much of an effort to get up and fetch a nightgown.

Although she felt deathly weary, sleep was elusive. Too much of what King had said haunted her as she stared into the half-darkness. He was right, he *was* an addiction. One taste of what he could give her and she was hooked.

But addicts did cure themselves and if it meant going through the pain of cold-turkey withdrawal that's what she would have to do. She resolved to get away from here completely, never see him or talk to him again and hope that it would be enough to get him out of her system.

But there was no chance of making her escape until they had finished the location shooting so she would have to keep as much distance between them as possible until then.

Tammy was at breakfast alone when Shan came into the dining room next morning. Her furtive glances over the top of the book she was ostensibly reading confirmed Shan's belief that she had helped Jason to set his trap last night. 'Good morning, Tammy,' she said evenly, helping herself to fruit juice and coffee from the sideboard and ignoring the selection of hot food.

'Good morning, Shan,' the teenager said with brittle gaiety. 'How did you sleep?'

'*We* slept very well, thank you,' King intervened smoothly, coming into the room behind Shan.

Tammy's smug expression was replaced by one of astonishment as she caught the plural and its implication. 'That ... that's good,' she stammered. She dropped her spoon into her cereal bowl with a clatter and stood up. 'Excuse me.'

King paused in the act of piling his plate with bacon and eggs, and turned to her. 'Where are you off to in such a hurry?'

'I ... I have to see Jason about ... about our scenes this morning.'

He set his plate down on the table. 'I'd rather you didn't see Jason just yet. I want to have a talk with him first.'

Tammy's mouth dropped open. 'But, Dad ...'

'Finish your breakfast,' he said ominously.

Subdued, she returned to her seat and hid behind the book again. Normally, King would have reminded her of her manners but this morning, he ignored the deliberate display of rudeness and calmly started on his breakfast. 'What are you up to this morning, Shan?' he asked with infuriating calmness.

She clenched her hands together under the table. 'We're shooting some scenes between Tammy and Jason around the billabong.' How could he be so calm when every nerve in her body was jumping at the mere sight of him, remembering the heights he had transported her to last night. Obviously it hadn't meant as much to him as it had to her, nor left such a lasting impression.

Of course, he had called himself an addiction. And there wasn't an addict in existence who loved the source of their addiction, or wouldn't do anything they could to be rid of it.

After an age, he finished his meal and stacked his plates ready for Mrs Gordon to clear away, then rose smoothly.

Shan followed him out into the hallway and tugged at his arm. 'What are you going to say to Jason?'

For the first time that morning, she provoked a glimmer of angry response. 'What do you expect? I'm going to send him packing right now.'

'But you can't do that.'

His frown deepened. 'Why the hell not? You said what happened last night was one-sided . . . unless of course, it wasn't.'

'Don't be ridiculous,' she snapped. 'I'm only thinking of the film. We've already shot too many of the station owner's scenes to replace him with another actor, even if we could find someone as good as Jason for the money he was willing to accept. In any case, he has a contract and could justifiably sue me for a fortune in damages. After all, it's only my word against his that I didn't encourage his advances. You had enough doubts so I can just imagine what a jury would think.'

'You have to admit, for a moment it did sound as though you wanted to have your cake and eat it.'

'It's not like that at all. I have no choice but to keep him around.'

He looked thoughtful. 'It seems none of us has a choice, have we?'

Before she could ask what he meant by this enigmatic remark, he disentangled her hand from his arm. 'I'm still going to have a talk with Cody.' He cut short her protest. 'Don't worry, I won't do anything to damage that famous profile.' With that, he walked off towards the sleeping wing.

When she went outside, the crew was loading the last of the gear on to the four-wheel-drive vehicles for transport to the billabong. 'Everything all right?' she asked Dave.

'All under control. As soon as our star puts in an appearance, we can be on our way.'

It was a very subdued-looking Jason Cody who joined them a short while later. Without a word to anyone, he climbed into the lead vehicle and sat staring moodily out of the window while the others dispersed to their cars.

Shan noticed that Tammy put as much distance between herself and Jason as was humanly possible and she smiled inwardly. It would be a long time before Tammy tried to recruit him as her co-conspirator again.

They set off down the winding bush track which was becoming daily more familiar, most of the outdoor sequences having been filmed in and around the waterhole.

By now they took its tranquil beauty almost for granted, although Shan felt that she would never have enough of the unique atmosphere. Much as she loved her busy city lifestyle, she felt more at home here in the bush than anywhere else.

How easy it would be to settle down here, she thought dreamily, then pulled her thoughts up sharply. There was only one way she could stay and that was by surrendering completely to King. However desirable she found the idea, Tammy would never permit it. And Shan wasn't masochistic enough to sentence herself to a lifetime of such misery.

Wild geese and ducks dotted the lagoon in such numbers that the water was black with them. When the convoy approached, the birds took off all together with a concerted flapping of wings, darkening the sun for a moment. Shan watched them go a little wistfully.

How free and unfettered they were.

'How often have you eaten roast duck?' Dave asked, coming up alongside her car. 'You were looking at the flock as if you'd like to join them.'

'I was, wasn't I?' She took his point. Even the wild birds had their problems.

They were shooting in a glade of paperbark trees, along a path edged with wild grasses, which led down to the edge of the billabong. It was a particularly attractive location and as she watched Jason and Tammy transform themselves into the likeable station owner, Ben Drysdale, and his daughter, Libby, she relaxed for the first time in many hours. If only she could freeze them in their present characters, how much simpler life would be.

The character of Libby was a pleasant, wide-eyed young woman whose only crime was that she fell in love with an aboriginal youth of whom her parents disapproved. That his tribal family also opposed the marriage formed the film's main conflict. It was Romeo and Juliet of the bush, and the romance had a special poignancy in this primeval setting.

'Look out, behind you!'

She jumped as the man King had assigned to the crew came rushing up to her, pushing her out of the way to get a clear shot at the water's edge. 'He took off when I shouted,' he said, lowering his weapon.

'What was it?' she asked, still shaken.

'A big saltie. He was sneaking up behind you while you stood here dreaming. You should know better than that, Mrs Falconer.'

'Shan, please,' she said automatically. He still remembered her from the early days of her marriage. 'I wasn't thinking, I suppose. Thanks for warning me.'

'If I had let you get eaten by a crocodile the boss

would've eaten me,' the man grinned and backtracked towards the group.

She followed him more slowly. The incident was a timely reminder that the outback, for all its beauty, was a place of hidden danger—like her relationship with King. No matter how she romanticised the involvement, it was still dangerous for her. Like all dangers, she would be wise not to let herself become complacent.

Not for the first time, work was her therapy. Luckily, her job as producer kept her so busy that by the time they broke for lunch, she had managed to avoid thinking about King once. Of course, she couldn't work at this pace for every minute of the day. Sooner or later there would be unguarded moments when he crept into her thoughts, but with luck she could keep them to a minimum.

Dave crossed the clearing and joined her in the shade of a paperbark. 'I don't know what's happened to Jason but I can't remember when he's been so co-operative,' he mused.

She knew exactly what had happened to Jason. After his talk with King this morning, he had no doubt decided that discretion was preferable to valour. For all Jason's workouts in the gym, King was by far the more muscular and she had no doubt who could come off best in a fight. But she couldn't say all that to Dave without explaining the background, so she shrugged. 'Maybe you should just enjoy it while it lasts.'

'Just what I was thinking.'

They ate their lunch in companionable silence for a while, then Dave set his lunch box aside. 'I've been hoping for a chance to talk to you, Shan.'

She smiled. 'My door is always open—metaphorically speaking out here of course—especially to you.'

'This isn't business. It's personal.'

Here we go again, she thought with more than a trace of amusement. She couldn't remember how many times Dave had opened a discussion with that line. His personal problems almost invariably concerned the current love of his life. 'What's her name?' she asked resignedly.

He looked startled. 'How did you know it was a girl?'

'I've known you a long time, Dave. We grew up in this business together, remember? I'm the nearest thing you have to a sister.'

Idly, he plucked at some strands of grass. 'Sometimes I wish you weren't such a good sister. We could have made a terrific team, you and I.'

She shook her head. 'No way. We're too much alike for one thing. And for another . . .'

'I know,' he interrupted glumly, 'you're married. Although you're going to do something about that, aren't you?'

This conversation was taking a dangerous turn. 'What do you mean?' she asked.

'Well, since you aren't living together any more, aren't you planning to get a divorce?'

She hadn't thought that far ahead yet, but it was how failed marriages usually ended up, she supposed. The thought of legally ending her marriage made her feel depressed, even though it was inevitable now. 'Even if I do get a divorce, I'll think twice about getting marriage again—to anyone.'

'Once bitten—right?'

'Something like that. In any case, we weren't talking about me. You said you had a problem?'

He sighed theatrically. 'I'm in love.'

'So what else is new?'

He looked hurt. 'This time it's serious. I'm in love

with her and she doesn't even acknowledge my existence.'

'All right, I'll bite. What's her name.'

He sat upright, propping his back against the tree trunk. 'That's more like it. It's Tammy.'

All trace of amusement left her face. 'You can't be serious—Tammy Falconer?'

'Your lovely stepdaughter. I know I'm not in her class but . . .'

'That's not the question. She's only eighteen, Dave—still a child.'

His answering frown told her this thought had already occurred to him. 'I know. But eighteen is legally adult these days, certainly old enough to know your own mind. Besides, I'm only twenty-four which is hardly in my dotage.'

She couldn't argue with his logic. She had been just eighteen herself when she first met King and he had made an indelible impression on her, eclipsing any other man in her life. So who was she to say that eighteen was too young to know your own mind? 'I'll grant you the age isn't a big problem—but what did you want me to do?'

'You're legally her stepmother. Would you have a talk with her, explain my finer points . . .'

She laughed hollowly. 'I'm sorry, Dave, but I can't.'

'There's no need to laugh. If I'm not good enough for her just say so and I'll clear off.'

'It's not that,' she said, sobering at once. 'But you're asking the wrong person. Tammy hates me. She can't wait to be rid of me.'

He squirmed uncomfortably against the tree. 'I'm sorry, Shan. I had no idea.'

'It's all right, nobody does. She's careful to be polite in front of others. But she has always resented me trying to fill her mother's shoes.'

Dave scrambled up and held out his hand to her. 'You're twice the woman Joanna Price ever was and somebody ought to tell Tammy so.'

Alarm brought the colour rushing to her cheeks. 'No! You mustn't say anything to her about me. But I wish you well on your own behalf. I think you'd be very good for her.'

'Let's hope she thinks so.' He dropped a light, brotherly kiss on her cheek. 'Thanks for letting me pour out my heart.'

'Touching, very touching,' came a cynical drawl. She stiffened as King joined them in the clearing. His outdoorsman's gait made him seem even taller and more commanding alongside Dave.

His unexpected appearance sent a chill of apprehension down her spine. 'King! Dave and I were just . . .'

Dave looked uncomfortable as he interrupted her. 'I think that's my exit cue.' He hurried off towards the camera crew who were loading gear on to the truck.

Suddenly she and King were alone in the clearing. 'It wasn't what you thought,' she said stiffly.

Unexpectedly, he burst into laughter. 'It's all right. I believe you.'

She stared at him, dumbfounded. 'You do?'

'Of course. After last night, there's no way that Cameron could satisfy you. You need a man, not a boy.'

Swiftly, he closed the distance between them and took her in his arms. 'This is what you need.' His mouth sought hers and claimed it with a fierce passion which sent tremors through her whole body.

Her first thought was of resistance, but it was like trying to stem a flood with a matchstick. Her need of him overcame everything else and she gave herself up to the bitter sweetness of being in his arms once more.

His lips were hot against hers and his tongue invaded her mouth with possessive confidence, setting up a fiery ache in the pit of her stomach. It took all of her strength to tear herself from his embrace.

As she pressed herself defensively against the tree trunk with her arms wrapped around her body, a smile played around the corners of his mouth. 'There's no escape. You're hooked on me and it's only a matter of time before you admit it.'

The fact that he was right only made her more conscious of the need to resist him while she still could. He thought he had her on some sort of sexual leash which he had only to tug at to bring her to heel. She injected all the scorn she could into her voice. 'You'd better prepare yourself for a long wait in that case. I've been getting along perfectly well without you for three years. What makes you think I can't go on doing it?'

He fixed his far-seeing gaze on her for a long moment before he answered. 'That was before I put the Falconer brand on you. Even if you stray, you will always be drawn back to me by that.'

Although the day was hot, she shivered. Even as he spoke she could feel the imprint of his lovemaking on her as surely as if the Double F brand had been burned into her skin.

'Stop it!' she ordered, as much for her active imagination as for his benefit. 'The way you lump me in with your cattle makes me expect to be hauled down to the mustering camp to be put under the branding iron with the rest of your herd.'

He tugged moodily at his chin. 'It's a thought. But I'd hate to disfigure that perfect skin of yours. Especially when I've already marked you just as effectively without leaving a scar.'

What made him think she had no scars? Just

because they weren't visible didn't mean they weren't there. After last night she would always carry the scar of his possession in her mind, if not on her body. 'I think this discussion has gone far enough,' she said stiffly. 'I have work to do even if you don't.'

'That's right, keep running away,' he said softly for her ears alone. 'You'll come back in the end.'

'You're so sure of yourself, aren't you?'

He grinned, making her want to slap that smug expression off his face. 'Shouldn't I be?'

She was drowning in the core of his personality. Could it be true? *Had* he branded her in some mysterious way which made it impossible for her to escape him? She told herself she was being fanciful. 'Occasionally, a horse you've broken surprises you by running off just when you think you've mastered him,' she said defiantly. She had seen this happen herself.

She had touched a nerve. Uncertainty flickered on his handsome features. 'There is such a thing as a horse which can't be broken,' he conceded.

'Or a spirit?' she flashed back. 'I might still surprise you yet.'

'And I may surprise you.'

'What do you mean?'

'I've been thinking about what you said last night—about Tammy.'

Hope fluttered like caged bird in her breast. 'And?'

'And I've decided to have a talk with her. But don't get your hopes too high,' he added quickly. 'I want to be very sure I'm doing the right thing before I say too much.'

She could hardly believe it. There was a chance for them after all! If he would only talk to Tammy and convince her that Joanna wasn't the paragon she believed in, then she might be willing to accept Shan as her stepmother. Shan brushed away the tears which sprang to her eyes at the prospect. 'Thank you, King.'

'Don't thank me yet,' he cautioned. 'I won't do anything which might hurt Tammy.'

'And I wouldn't expect you to. But I really believe it's for her own good.' A great wave of tenderness flooded through her. She knew how difficult this was for him, and the fact that he had agreed to talk to Tammy about Joanna told Shan that he *did* care for her after all. Maybe now she could tell him how she felt about him. 'King, I . . .'

There were interrupted by a call from the camera truck. 'Miss Penrose! Can you come over here?'

What now? She looked helplessly at King. 'I've got to go.'

'I'll come with you.'

Before she could forestall him he strode ahead of her towards the waiting crew. 'What's the problem?'

A cameraman called John stepped forward. 'It was my fault, Miss Penrose. I didn't know she was so touchy.'

She put a hand to her head. 'Just a minute. Who is touchy and about what?'

'It's Tammy,' Dave said grimly. 'John was rehearsing a scene with her and she was being difficult so he said something about her being as awkward to work with as her mother. It developed into a shouting match which ended when she grabbed one of the horses and rode off.'

'Oh, no!' breathed Shan. She turned to King. 'Do you have any idea where she could have gone?'

He clenched and unclenched his hands, anger staining his face with dark colour. 'You bitch!' he railed at Shan. 'You just couldn't keep your mouth shut, could you?'

She stared at him in disbelief. Surely he didn't think she had engineered this. 'King, I swear . . .' she began but he cut her off.

'Save your explanations. My daughter is riding around out there in God-knows-what state of mind. Anything could happen to her.'

'I'm sure she'll be all right,' Dave said tautly.

King's expression was scathing. 'What would you know about it, born and bred in a city.'

'I'm sorry, sir, I only meant . . .'

King ignored him, turning to the cameraman. 'Which way did she go?'

John indicated the direction and King swung himself on to his horse. 'She can't have gone far.' To his stockman, he snapped, 'Radio the homestead and have them send Jack Callahan out here, then the two of you follow my tracks. If I don't have any luck, maybe an aboriginal tracker will.'

'When you find her please tell her I didn't mean what I said about her mother,' intervened the cameraman, 'I wish to hell I'd kept my mouth shut.'

King's flinty gaze fastened on Shan, standing pale-faced beside the camera truck, too shocked to move. 'When I find her, a lot of people will be wishing the same thing.'

CHAPTER SEVEN

'SHE'LL be all right, Shan. Tammy knows this property like the back of her hand.'

She wished she had Dave's confidence. He didn't know about Tammy's attempted suicide or her recent threat to try again. She debated whether to tell him then decided that there was time enough for that if anything came of his interest in the girl. 'I suppose you're right,' she sighed and forced herself to sit down, although it was an effort not to jump up and start pacing again.

'That's better,' Dave smiled. 'God knows, I'm as worried about her as you are but I just have this feeling that everything will be all right. King will soon find her and bring her back.'

Yes, if anyone could find her, he could. And he had his aboriginal tracker on standby, a man whom the Northern Territory police often called in to help locate missing people. He had an uncanny ability to follow a trail which was invisible to anyone else.

'If only I hadn't started that business about her mother,' John said miserably.

Rona patted him on the shoulder. 'If it hadn't been you it would have been one of us. We've all worked with Joanna Price and we know what she was like. Working with her daughter, sooner or later someone was bound to make comparisons.'

If only King would see it like that, Shan brooded. But she remembered too vividly the savage look in his face when he made it clear that she would regret discussing Joanna with anyone. He would never believe that the cameraman had spoken on impulse, little realising the damage he was doing.

If anyone was to blame, it was King himself. He was the one who insisted on building a fantasy image of Joanna in Tammy's mind. Joanna's publicity machine had worked overtime to build the nice-girl image which was the one Tammy cherished but she wouldn't be able to work in the film industry for long without finding out the truth. Surely King could see that?

She twisted her handkerchief in nerveless fingers. 'How long has it been?'

Dave glanced at the grandfather clock. 'It took us an hour to drive back to the homestead, and we've been sitting here for another two—three hours altogether.'

'Then why isn't there some news?' she asked in anguish.

Dave gave her a curious look. 'Is there something about all this that you haven't told us?'

She averted her eyes. 'No, of course not. Tammy's just ... highly strung, that's all. She's liable to do something silly.'

His relief was immediately apparent. 'As long as that's all you're concerned about. I just thought there might be something more to it.'

'Tea's ready if anyone's interested,' Mrs Gordon said from the doorway. Her face was drawn and strained and she wiped her hands repeatedly on a spotless apron.

'No thanks, I'm not hungry,' volunteered Shan. 'But the rest of you go and eat. I'll have something later.'

Reluctantly the others drifted towards the dining room leaving Shan alone. Relieved to be free from their scrutiny, she resumed her restless pacing up and down. They had all been wonderful about Tammy's disappearance, putting it down to temperament mostly. In fact, by running away, Tammy had only added fuel to the inevitable comparisons between herself and Joanna Price. Her behaviour today certainly wouldn't win her any points if she wanted to continue working in the film industry.

Tired out at last, Shan curled up on a corner of the sofa and tucked her feet underneath her, hardly noticing as the shadows in the room lengthened. It was too bad that John had chosen today to argue with Tammy about her mother. Now it would be much harder for King to convince Tammy of the truth. Already, he thought Shan had done some damage by jumping the gun—although the incident had been in no way her fault.

What if she couldn't make King believe that? She had to, otherwise there was no future for them at all. The next step would be the divorce Dave had foreshadowed during lunch. Their discussion seemed almost prophetic now.

Still, the thought of legally ending her ties with King made her want to weep. Last night he had said he made her complete, which was tragically true. Without him she would be leaving a part of herself behind at Faraway. But surely that was better than losing all of herself by staying?

'Wake up, Shan, King's back!'

Groggily, she pulled herself upright on the sofa as Dave shook her gently by the shoulder. 'I must have dozed off. Has he got Tammy with him?'

'I think he rode in alone but we'll have to wait and ask him. There's no point in imagining the worst.'

They looked up expectantly as King strode into the living room. His face was lined and haggard and his clothes were caked with bulldust from his long ride. 'You can stop worrying, I found her,' he said shortly.

There was a visible relaxation of tension around the room. 'Where is she?' Dave asked for all of them.

'She was holed up in the old homestead. I should have guessed she'd go there. It's where she used to hide when she was upset as a child.'

'So you brought her back with you?' Shan prompted.

He looked at her with thinly veiled contempt which told her he still believed this was her fault. 'No, I didn't. She said she would come back when she was ready, and she's a bit too old to throw across my saddle so I had to agree. I left Jack camped nearby to keep an eye on her. I'll ride out there again tomorrow to see if she's ready to come home.'

He looked around at the assembled crew. 'You can all go get some sleep now, the drama's over.' Passing a hand over his eyes, he added gruffly, 'Thanks for sticking around.'

'We were all worried,' Rona explained. 'And we're very glad she's safe. Good night all.'

They chorused their good nights and trooped off to the guest quarters. Jason had waited in the background to hear the news then had left quietly to go to his room. Since King's discussion with him over his treatment of Shan, he had been a model of decorum, raising a few eyebrows among the crew who noted the change.

Mrs Gordon came in, her face wreathed in smiles. 'I'm so relieved that she's all right, Mr Falconer. Can I get you some supper now? You must be starving.'

He forced a smile. 'Thanks, Mrs Gordon, but it's time you got some rest, too. Shan will fix me something if I need it later.'

The housekeeper undid her apron and rolled it up. 'It has been a trying day so I'll be glad of an early night. You're sure you don't mind, Shan?'

It was an effort to keep her tone light. 'You heard the man, Mrs Gordon,' she said in a brittle voice.

When the housekeeper had gone, he fixed her with a steely gaze. 'I hope it won't be too much trouble fixing a snack for your husband.' He emphasised the last word.

'That's what wives are supposed to do for husbands, isn't it?' she parried, thinking at the same time that husbands were supposed to respect and *trust* their wives. He had shown little signs of doing either.

'Aren't you going to tell me how glad you are that Tammy's safe?' he asked drily.

'Well of course I am.' What did he expect her to say? 'You make it sound as if I was glad she was missing.'

'I don't know what to think about you any more,' he said in such a dispirited tone that her heart went out to him, in spite of his readiness to condemn her.

To defuse her instinct to go to him, she turned towards the kitchen. 'I'll fix you that meal.'

'Sandwiches will do, thanks. Could you bring them to my room? I'd like to wash some of this grime off.'

As soon as she heard his footsteps disappearing down the corridor to his room, she slumped against the kitchen counter. It had taken all of her self-control not to wrap him in her arms and soothe some of his hurt away with her kisses. Yet as long as he believed she had put John up to baiting Tammy about her mother, she would be a fool to give in to him. How could he believe she could do such a thing?

Mechanically, she set her hands to the task of making the sandwiches while her mind agonised over what she should do next. If he refused to give her the benefit of the doubt, she would have no choice but to leave. And if she was to escape with anything of her identity intact she would have to make sure there was no repetition of last night.

If she could only maintain her distance from him she would lessen the effect of his attraction. Remembering her vow to kick her addiction to him 'cold-turkey', she knew it was the only way. In time, like all brands, the mark he had left on her would dull and blur and she would have only a bittersweet memory. As long as she kept feeding the addiction by succumbing to his embraces, she would only increase her need of him.

How logical and sensible it all sounded. Yet when she took the tray of sandwiches to his room and was greeted by him wrapped only in a towel which left his magnificent chest and muscular legs bare, her composure was very nearly shattered.

Jerkily, she set the tray down and started to leave. 'Come back,' he commanded.

Hating herself, she froze. 'Yes? Was there something else?'

'Stop sounding like a damned parlour maid,' he growled. 'You and I have to talk.'

'There's nothing to talk about as long as you've tried and condemned me in advance.'

He settled himself on the side of the bed. 'Stop being so dramatic for a moment. I can understand what you were trying to do.' He bit into the sandwich and the sight of his bent head and even teeth cutting a neat half circle out of the bread almost destroyed her resolve. She reminded herself that he still believed she had put John up to discussing Joanna with Tammy.

'It's kind of you to be so understanding,' she said sarcastically. 'Except that it's entirely misplaced.' The scepticism in his face told her there was no point in continuing to defend herself. Her shoulders slumped. 'It's been a long day. I just want to get to bed.'

It was the wrong thing to say, she realised as soon as

she saw the gleam of passion in his eyes. 'That's exactly what I had in mind.'

She shook her head decisively. 'No thank you.'

'No thank you,' he mimicked. 'You say that so convincingly, but I know what you're thinking.'

How could he know that with every fibre of her being she yearned to creep into the bed beside him and snuggle close to him for warmth and comfort. But how could she as long as he refused to trust her? 'You think you know me so well, yet you can believe I put John up to telling Tammy about Joanna,' she said stiffly.

His face darkened. 'You have to admit, it *was* quite a coincidence that it should have happened just after our discussion.'

'Well it *was* just coincidence,' she said hotly. 'You must realise that sooner or later, something like this was bound to happen.'

'You made quite sure of it, didn't you?'

What was the use? 'Oh, think what you like, you will anyway,' she said on a note of exasperation, adding tensely, 'Are you still going to have a talk with her?'

'How can I? You saw the way she reacted today. The whole truth would destroy her.'

So that was that. Through a haze of misery, she saw her hopes for their shared future dissolve into nothing. But even as she faced this prospect, his eyes clouded with desire and he reached for her. Despairingly, she eluded him. 'No, King, I can't. Not after all that's happened today.'

'Look, I know we have our differences. But that doesn't stop me wanting you—or you wanting me. You can't deny that you do.'

'I wouldn't try to deny it. But I can't separate physical love and mutual respect, the way you seem to do.'

'I've always respected you, Shan,' he defended himself.

'You have a strange way of showing it.'

He folded his arms across his chest. 'What would you have me do?'

Her voice came out as a subdued whisper. 'Trust me.'

Slowly, he replaced the sandwich plate on the tray and brushed crumbs from the bed while she sat tensely, waiting for his response. 'Trust you,' he said at last. 'Funny, but that's what Joanna asked of me—and I gave it to her. She repaid me by having one affair after another. Tammy wanted me to trust her, too. So I sent her to school in another state and she obliged me by taking up a profession she knew I despised. After that sort of treatment, a man tends to run low on trust.'

The dresser mirror reflected the silent appeal in her eyes. 'You can't hold me responsible for all the faults of my gender.'

He laughed hollowly. 'That would be unfair, I agree. But then your own track record speaks fro itself. Or don't you count running away from our marriage without so much as a word or a note as a betrayal of trust?'

She stared at him, aghast. 'But I did leave you a note, on the windscreen of the car I borrowed to drive to the airport.'

'I never received it. We had a tropical storm the night you left. It must have washed the note away. In it, I suppose you told me how sorry you were that things hadn't worked out,' he said sourly.

'No. I . . . I said I wanted time to think.'

His expression was sneering. 'You needed three years to think?'

She turned away from him. 'I wrote to you during those years. You never answered.'

'There didn't seem to be any point. You made your feelings clear the day you walked out of here.'

'What's the use? We're just not suited to each other so why keep trying?'

He moved deliberately towards her, his eyes dark with unmistakable desire. 'Oh but we are, Shan. That's why you came to Faraway the first time, even though you still believed I was married. And whether you admit it or not, it's why you came back this time.'

With a muffled cry, she scrabbled at the door handle and twisted it open, then fled to her own room.

Breathing heavily, she leaned against her own door half-expecting him to come after her. But the only sounds she could hear were of him moving restively around his room.

Gradually, her breathing returned to normal and she sank on to a chair. She couldn't take much more of this. He only knew one way of communicating with her and that she must resist at all costs. She didn't want his love any more—she craved it, and that was a different thing altogether.

Next morning she arose having slept little but feeling much more clear-headed than she had in months. King wanted her physically—he made no secret of that. But as long as there was no trust between them, they had nothing.

Maybe Shakespeare's 'marriage of true minds' was a pipe dream. If so, she intended to go on dreaming. The rest of that sonnet was just as appropriate—'Love is not love which alters when it alteration finds.' To Shakespeare and to her it was 'an ever-fixed mark, that looks on tempests and is never shaken'. King's love for her was much too easily shaken to endure.

He was morose and distant during breakfast and over coffee, announced that he was driving to the old homestead to collect Tammy.

'Mind if I come along?' asked Dave. 'From the sound of the place, it would make an ideal location for the wedding scene which we'll be filming next week— that's if you have no objections, sir?'

'None at all,' King agreed mildly. 'You'll come too, Shan, of course?'

It was the last thing she wanted to do but Dave had left her little leeway to refuse, since she would have to make the final decision about the location. 'Yes, I'll come. I'll ride with Dave.'

King said nothing to contradict this but when they went outside to the waiting vehicles, she found that Dave had been allocated the camera truck. His vehicle was loaded with gear so she had no option but to join King in his four-wheel-drive. 'Couldn't we have taken the other Land-Rover?' she asked as she settled into the car beside King, leaving a wide space between them.

He looked at the space without comment. 'The rest of your crew have taken it down to the billabong,' he explained. 'Since you gave them a day off today, they asked if they could barrow the cars for a picnic. I warned them against going swimming there.'

And who was supposed to warn her? she thought bitterly. 'You seem to have thought of everything,' she said grimly.

His answering smile was as warm as a crocodile's. 'I usually do.'

It was as if he had sensed her plan to put as much distance as possible between them and was determined to thwart her. If he could read her intentions as clearly as that, it would make things much more difficult for her.

She brooded on the problem during the long drive across the grassy savannah plains but still hadn't thought of a solution by the time they reached the old homestead. King told her it was located in a floodway which was cut off from everything by floodwaters during the Wet, as its first occupants had found to their dismay. Luckily, the building itself was on sufficiently high ground that they were safe until the water receded, after which they had wisely decided to build elsewhere. King's present homestead had been built on the new site.

The original building was mostly made of corrugated iron sheets, partly lined inside and with a wide verandah all around. As they approached it, Shan could see that it had been kept in surprisingly good repair.

'It's used by the stockmen when they have to spend nights out this way mending fences, repairing windmills and the like so we keep it stocked with tinned food and sleeping bags,' King explained. 'Tammy used to spend nights here during her school vacations.'

This explained why the teenager seemed none the worse for her adventures. Apart from being in need of a wash, she was surprisingly cheerful when she came out on to the verandah to greet them.

'I believe you owe everyone an apology for your behaviour yesterday,' King said by way of a greeting.

She pouted prettily. 'If you say so, Dad.' She fluttered her silky eyelashes at Dave who reddened. 'You will forgive me, won't you, Dave?'

The young director looked as if he would forgive her anything when she acted like that. 'There's nothing to forgive,' he said brusquely. 'We all have our off-days, as long as it's over now.'

'Oh, it's over,' she assured him. 'I over-react a bit sometimes, I know.'

Which was the understatement of the year, Shan thought sourly. She had stayed in the background through all this, not wanting to upset Tammy again by her presence. The teenager gave no signs of noticing her, for which Shan was glad.

'I'd like a word alone with Tammy, if you don't mind,' King requested.

At once, Dave retreated to the parked vehicles where Shan waited in the pool of shade they provided. 'She's got nerve, I'll say that for her,' he said, his tone full of grudging admiration. 'If King Falconer was my father, I'd be quaking in my shoes if I had to face him after yesterday's performance.'

'She probably is,' Shan observed. 'I'd say all that nonchalance is just bravado. But then, I'm forgetting you're prejudiced where Tammy's concerned.'

He grinned ruefully. 'I'm a glutton for punishment, I guess.' He straightened. 'While those two have a heart-to-heart, I might as well check the rest of the place out. It looks ideal for the wedding scene which we will be filming as soon as the billabong sequences are completed.'

Shan had been thinking the same thing. 'It will save us a fortune if we don't have to build a homestead set. I didn't expect this one to be in such good repair.'

Notepad in hand, Dave set off to check out the building's possibilities and Shan settled back against the truck. Reflexively, she tensed as King came over to her. 'Is everything all right?'

He squinted against the sun's glare and eased his hat further back on to his head. 'You told me once that there was nothing between you and Dave Cameron, right?'

'Yes. And that's still true.'

'Did you know Cameron and Tammy are interested in one another?'

'I didn't know it was mutual but I know Dave cares about her,' she said cautiously. What was he getting at?

'If you knew that much, why the hell were you putting obstacles in their way?'

The attack was so unexpected that she reeled back as if he had struck her physically. 'Is that what Tammy thinks I've been doing?'

'Yes. That's one of the reasons why she flared up and ran away yesterday. She's been trying to catch Cameron's eye but it seems that every time she does, you annex him for lunch or a chat or some such.'

'That's ridiculous. We work together. Consultations are part of our routine.'

His eyes narrowed. 'What about lunches and little *têtes à têtes* in the corridors?' Before she could respond, he plunged on. 'At least it would explain why you want Tammy off the scene.'

She stared at him, open-mouthed and it was a minute or two before she found her voice. 'You can't think I'm jealous of Tammy?' she asked.

'What else am I to think? You profess to have no interest in Cameron and yet you don't want Tammy to have him, either.'

'I'm not in love with Dave, I'm . . .' She almost said she was in love with King but bit the words back just in time.

'You're what—sleeping with him?' he supplied contemptuously. 'Is that why you refuse to share my bed any more?'

'I've only shared it once,' she reminded him. 'And I've no intention of sharing it again—yours or anybody's,' she added pointedly.

'Once was enough to prove to me that you're no nun,' he threw at her. 'But I didn't think you'd stoop to hurting an innocent girl to satisfy your needs.'

'You can't think I started that business about Joanna just to get Tammy out of the way?' she demanded.

'Can you give me a better explanation?' he derided. 'Oh, come on, Shan, you've had it in for Tammy since the day you met her.'

Tears of vexation clouded her vision and she shook her head to be rid of them. 'You're wrong,' she breathed. 'I know there's no way I can make you believe me, but I look on Dave Cameron as a brother. We grew up in the film business together. That's all there is to it. If you must know,' she added recklessly, 'he had lunch with me yesterday to ask me to put in a good word for him with Tammy.'

All at once, the strain of the last few days overcame her and the tears brimmed over in earnest. She huddled against the side of the truck, her face averted.

'Oh God, Shan, I'm sorry, don't cry,' he pleaded, taking her in his arms. She held herself stiffly against him as he drew out a handkerchief and blotted her streaming eyes. 'I believe you. I guess I was the one who was jealous, thinking you were in love with Dave Cameron.'

She stared up at him in amazement. 'You were jealous?'

'Yes. When Tammy said you two were always together . . .'

'But I've told you there's nothing to be jealous of,' she persisted, trying to pull away from him.

He held her tightly. 'I know. But it always seems as if you have love enough to spare for everyone but me.'

This time, she did manage to twist free. 'I've told you what's wrong between us.'

He sighed heavily. 'I know—Joanna.' His eyes flashed a mute appeal. 'But you must see why I can't tell Tammy the truth now, not after the way she reacted yesterday?'

'All I can see is an impossible situation with no solution,' she returned tonelessly. 'You can't tell

Tammy the truth and until you do, she will never let me be a part of your life.'

He clicked his tongue in exasperation and seemed about to say something more, then turned abruptly and strode off. He reached a cluster of boulders which towered higher than a man, and stopped there, his back to her.

She longed to go after him but it would only prolong the intolerable situation between them. He seemed to think she should ignore Tammy's behaviour and maybe she should. But he didn't know how hard it was to put up with Tammy's innuendoes day after day, while he was away. She just couldn't go through that again.

Dave came back, his expression buoyant. 'I don't know what King said to Tammy but it seems she feels the same way about me as I do about her.'

'So he tells me,' Shan said drily.

'You don't seem very pleased about it.'

She forced a smile to her lips. 'Of course I am. I'm delighted for you Dave. I hope you and Tammy can make a go of it.'

'King seems to think we can. Tammy says he's already given us a sort of blessing.'

'In what way?'

He grinned. 'She says he's completely changed his attitude towards the film industry, since we've been here. He told Tammy that he's considering funding other films in future.'

This was news to Shan. Considering how negative King had been when her company first arrived here, it was a major change indeed. 'I wonder what brought that about,' she mused.

'I don't know. Tammy says it must be because she and I look like teaming up. Apparently King says it wouldn't be the first time a husband had produced films as a vehicle for his wife.'

Shan's spirits sank. So that was how it was to be. If Dave married Tammy, King evidently intended to set his son-in-law up in his own production company, making films in which Tammy would star. She didn't have the heart to spoil Dave's jubilant mood by telling him that he had just hammered the last nail into the coffin of their marriage, so she said, 'That sounds like a good idea.'

He looked puzzled. 'I thought you'd be all for King getting into the film scene.'

Once she would have been deliriously happy about such a prospect. But now it was too late. The idea of having Tammy constantly involved in their lives even after she was married, gave Shan no joy at all.

'Did I say something wrong?' Dave quizzed her.

'No, of course not. It's very good news. With King's money, he could make a real contribution to the Australian film industry.'

Dave frowned. 'I don't think he plans to be personally involved, just as a backer.'

'Well whatever he has in mind, I'm sure it will be splendid. He has a way of doing anything he undertakes to the utmost.'

She left a bewildered Dave standing in the shade of the truck and wandered around to the back of the homestead, out of sight of the others. What did King want from her? Gratitude that she was to share a small corner of his life while he kept the lion's share for Tammy? He didn't even have the grace to tell her his plans himself, letting Dave pass the news on second-hand from Tammy.

So King saw himself in the role of film mogul. It didn't surprise her. He had always been the entrepreneurial type so the risk in film investment should suit him very well.

It would certainly suit Tammy. Not many actresses

enjoyed the luxury of having films created exclusively
to showcase their talents. Silently Shan wished them
all well. It was fortunate that she had already decided
on her own course of action. This morning's events
had only confirmed the rightness of her plans.

Luckily, they had only two major scenes still to film
at Faraway after the billabong shots were completed—
the wedding scene and a buffalo stampede. After that,
she would be free to return to Sydney.

'Shan, where are you?' came King's unmistakable
tones.

She debated whether to answer then decided that
she was entitled to these few minutes alone. King must
know the impact his news would have on her, since he
was well aware of how she felt about Tammy.

He came around the corner towards her. 'There you
are. Did Dave tell you my idea?'

'He said you were thinking of backing some more
films,' she said dully.

'I thought you'd be happy about it,' he said his tone
injured.

'I am—our film industry needs all the help it can
get,' she confirmed, her eyes bright with unshed tears.
She wished she could get out of here and shed them in
private, where he wouldn't see them.

But he wasn't letting her get away so lightly. 'And
what do you need?' he asked huskily.

You, she thought miserably. But mindful of her vow
to keep her distance, she said as lightly as she could,
'You can't buy a career for Tammy—or for anyone
else.'

'Is that what you think I'm trying to do?'

'Well isn't it?' What else did he call it, setting up his
prospective son-in-law in a film business so he could
ensure his daughter stardom?

That it would also ensure she was a constant thorn

in Shan's side, didn't seem to have occurred to him. 'I'd better be getting back,' she said evasively.

For a moment she thought he was going to block her passage but he stepped aside at the last moment. 'Still running away, aren't you?' he said sorrowfully. 'I thought I'd discovered a way to interest you in staying.'

Even she wasn't as selfless as that. 'Nice try,' she said with deliberate flippancy and felt as if she'd been stabbed when she saw him wince. She steeled herself against weakening. 'Remember the horse which can't be broken?' she prompted.

'Yes. But what . . .'

'You're looking at her.' With a heart which felt as if it was breaking but with her head held determinedly high, she walked back to the car.

CHAPTER EIGHT

IN the month they had been working at Faraway the crew had established a routine. As soon as breakfast was over everyone trooped out to the waiting convoy of four-wheel-drive vehicles and the laden camera truck. Today, they were filming the all-important wedding scene.

Without looking, Shan climbed into the lead vehicle and snapped on her seatbelt. 'Good morning, Dave.'

'Good morning, Shan,' came a soft voice.

At once she reached for the seatbelt fastening but the car was already jolting forwards. 'What are you doing here?' she demanded. 'I thought Dave was driving me.'

King smiled lazily. 'Well you thought wrong. He wanted to drive with Tammy so I volunteered to be your driver.'

'That's very big of you,' she hissed, trying to ignore her racing pulses and thudding heartbeat, symptoms she was used to experiencing whenever she was within feet of him. Until now, she had been able to keep out of his way quite successfully. She didn't want to start duelling with him now when the end of the project was in sight. 'Haven't you got a station to run?'

'I've also got a good team to help me run it,' he reminded her. 'Unlike certain people, I do have the knack of delegating responsibility.'

The hairs on the back of her neck rose slightly at the implied criticism. 'Are you suggesting that I don't?'

'Well I haven't seen you take any time off since you got here,' he observed. 'You're looking decidedly run-down these days.'

'It's kind of you to be so concerned about my welfare, but I assure you it isn't necessary.'

He chuckled throatily. 'Oh but it is. You are my wife, after all.'

'A fact I would prefer to forget,' she bridled.

'But a fact, nevertheless.'

'One I intend to do something about as soon as I return to Sydney,' she retorted.

She saw his hands tighten their grip on the steering wheel. 'I wondered when you'd get around to mentioning divorce. I won't agree.'

She looked away, pretending rapt interest in the groves of pandanus through which they were driving. 'I don't need your concurrence any more. The law is a lot more civilised these days.'

'But couples are still required to live apart for a fixed period to prove that the marriage is over,' he reminded her.

She stiffened. 'And what do you call the last three years?'

He nodded. 'That was a separation, undoubtedly. But you're forgetting that we've been . . . what's the legal word . . . cohabiting since you came here.'

She shot him a look of alarm. 'We have not been cohabiting, as you call it. We've slept together once— and *only* once, but surely . . .'

'The defence rests,' he said quietly.

This was a complication she hadn't thought about. Damn him and his seductive manner. If she hadn't let him coerce her into bed with him that one night she would have ample grounds for divorcing him. And she wouldn't have the haunting memory of that night to make her wonder whether she was doing the right thing.

Suddenly the car swerved on the rough bush track and she had to grab the doorhandle to save herself from being thrown sideways. When the dust cleared she looked behind them and was surprised to see the rest of the convoy continuing on in a different direction. 'What are you doing?'

'We're taking a little detour,' he said mildly. 'Don't worry, the others know we've gone.'

Don't worry! It was easy for him to say. 'Turn this car around right now,' she ordered. 'I haven't time for this. There's the wedding scene to set up. Without me . . .'

'Without you, Rona and Dave will manage very well,' he interrupted. 'I told you it will do you good to take a couple of hours off.'

Her first impulse was to make such a fuss that he had no choice but to turn the car around, but the prospect of a few hours free from responsibility was undeniably attractive.

She had awoken this morning feeling terrible, putting it down to a combination of overwork and the emotional strain of being with King again. She decided to give in gracefully. 'Where are you taking me?'

He gave her a gratified glance. 'That's more like it. You've never seen a buffalo round-up, have you?'

'No, but I've always wanted to.' Just in time, she curbed her enthusiasm. It would be just like King to plan this expedition to try to change her mind about leaving. He knew how much she loved this wild country. 'It will be something to remember when I'm back in Sydney,' she told him.

In the driving mirror, she saw his mouth tighten into a hard line. 'I'm not giving up yet, Shan.'

Since she didn't want to encourage this line of conversation, she concentrated on the wide grassy plains around them. In the distance, a brolga danced and near to them, a goanna reared up on its short bent

legs and ran away from them with a lurching motion
which reminded her of a child's wind-up toy.

King steered a careful path through the grey-green
scrub, avoiding the marshy areas where big black
boars with evil tusks and even more evil tempers
snuffled around.

They came on the first of the buffaloes grazing
quietly in a clearing fringed by pandanus palms. Shan
recognised the big bull by his massive backward-
curving horns. The cows with their gracefully
upswept horns followed stolidly behind the bull. As
soon as the car approached the bull and his harem
bolted for the shelter of the trees.

Beyond the marshy country they came upon a series
of immense fences built between the natural cliff
barriers which hemmed in the buffalo plains. Shan
heard the activity before she saw it. Then ahead of
them was the spectacle of stockmen on horseback and
truck, chasing small buffalo into the funnel made by
the fences and then into a narrow high-walled gully
from which there was no escape.

In the gully, another group of men in an old army
blitz truck herded the animals on to the back of a
waiting cattle truck.

'It looks dangerous,' she mused, watching intently
from their safe vantage point atop a small cliff.

'It is,' King assured her. 'Those animals weigh a
couple of tons each and their horns are all business.
We pioneered a lot of the methods we're using here
and most of the knowledge was acquired through
blood, sweat and tears.'

A shudder shook her as she remembered seeing him
lying helplessly under the hooves of the grey brumby
in the breaking yard. How much more must he and his
men have endured to perfect this method of rounding
up and taming the wild buffaloes? She reminded

herself that she wasn't supposed to feel anything for him any more, especially not compassion. Damn him! He had no doubt calculated the effect this sight would have on her, when he decided to bring her here.

'Very interesting,' she said with deliberate coolness.

'I'm glad it amuses you,' he said angrily and gunned the engine into life.

They followed the now-laden cattle truck to a specially built holding yard. Since no ordinary pen would hold the powerful animals, King had designed a fence no buffalo could break. Posts the size of tree trunks were bedded deep into the ground and arranged in a fifty-yard diameter circle. Rails for the fence were made from logs a foot thick and held by huge bolts and thick fencing wire. A narrow crush in which the animals could be held for inspection was built from old railway lines set in massive upright posts.

King explained all this as they watched the truck being backed into the yard. The only way the buffaloes could be induced off the vehicle was to bounce an old tyre from a rope across the open back of the truck. The bellowing animals charged this and found themselves in the yard. All their attempts to break out were futile, although the ground trembled under their repeated charges.

'It's hard to believe that such fierce beasts can ever be tamed,' she observed.

'Don't forget that they were descended from domestic water buffaloes brought to Australia from Indonesia in the 1800s as working beasts. When they were no longer needed, they were turned loose. The herds we have now started with those few animals.

'All it takes to tame them is to yard them like this for a week or so, then we turn them out into an ordinary paddock fenced with wire draped with hessian. By then, they're so brainwashed that they think anything man-made is buffalo-proof. They don't even try to break down the fences.'

'Why didn't anybody think of farming them before?' she asked, forgetting for a moment that she didn't want to seem too enthusiastic.

'Too dangerous. The first people who tried to farm them didn't realise that you can't out-fight them. You have to outwit them.' He chuckled softly. 'After a week or so getting them used to people and horses, we let them graze further afield. You should see these great beasts coming home to this yard at night.'

She looked at him in astonishment. 'They what?'

'They come back meek as you like. They think this is their sleeping camp. We encourage them to come home by bulldozing buffalo "roads" between the sleeping camps and the stands of irrigated lucerne we provide for grazing.'

'You could tame just about anything,' she said in genuine admiration.

Instead of being pleased by her praise he looked grim. 'Not quite anything,' he said flatly. 'There's one filly I haven't had any success at all with.'

She cursed herself for opening the way to this discussion. 'It won't work, King,' she said, deciding to tackle him head-on. 'I'm still leaving as soon as the film is completed.'

'You can't leave, I need you here,' he said thickly, his hand sliding along the back of the car seat.

She tensed as his fingers twined themselves in the hair at the base of her neck. His touch aroused an aching sensation deep in the pit of her stomach.

Sensing the danger, she shrugged his hand away. If she let him make love to her she was lost and she had a feeling he knew it. 'We've seen your buffalo. Can I get back to work now?' she said firmly.

At once, he dropped his hand to his side and sat for a moment in stony silence, then started the engine. 'As you like.'

The hostility between them was almost tangible as they drove back to the old homestead. On the way he handled the car as if it was a personal enemy, changing gears so violently that the car ground out a protest. Disregarding the rutted road, he aimed the car straight ahead until she thought her teeth would be jolted loose from her head.

She endured the punishing ride without protest. Better that he should take out his frustration on the driving than on her. If he chose to take her now, in this isolated place, there would be nothing she could do to stop him and if they made love even once more, she might not have the strength to leave as she knew she must.

They reached the homestead in record time and Shan tried to appear cool and calm as she stepped out of the car. 'Thanks for the ride,' she said politely.

Without answering, he slammed the vehicle into gear again and drove off in a flurry of bulldust.

'What was his hurry?' asked Rona, coming up to her.

She shrugged. 'How should I know?' To forestall any further questions, she flickered a glance over Rona's clipboard. 'How's it going?'

If Rona noticed the swift change of subject she chose to ignore it. 'Very well,' she said briskly. 'I managed to recruit all the extras we need from among the townspeople of Katherine. Once they discovered that we needed Victorian costumes, they came up with the most marvellous stuff out of trunks and attics.'

'That's wonderful news.' For the first time, Shan took a proper look at the crowd of extras milling around Dave. Their lovingly preserved outfits looked perfectly in place against the background of the old homestead.

Many of them had turned the day into a picnic, bringing along spouses and children and laden wicker picnic baskets to enjoy during a break in filming. The mood was happy and relaxed. 'You've done a good job,' she told Rona.

Her assistant looked pleased. 'Don't stop now. Honestly, I enjoyed it. They were all so eager to be in a real film. Pity Equity insists we only hire union members for the speaking parts.'

'I know. But we wouldn't want the film black-listed before it's released.' They both knew how strict the actors' union was about protecting the jobs of its members. They were lucky Equity had allowed them to hire as many non-actors as they had. 'Where's the bride?' she asked, missing Tammy.

'Over at the make-up van. She looks enchanting in her period wedding gown. I hope we don't need too many takes because we only have a half-dozen spare dresses.'

Rona was referring to the moment in the wedding scene when 'Libby's' aboriginal suitor interrupted the wedding and snatched the bride away. In the script, the girl went willingly because she had never wanted to marry her neighbour's son, only agreeing to placate her father.

The wedding was to be followed by a thrilling chase through the bush, as the father hunted the fleeing couple. At that point, the wedding gown would have to become dirty and dishevelled, but for now it had to look pristine through as many takes as the wedding scene demanded.

At that moment, a wave of nausea engulfed Shan and she staggered slightly. Worriedly, Rona supported her. 'Are you feeling all right?'

Shan straightened although it was an effort to do so. 'I'm fine. It was probably the rough drive to get here which upset me.'

'I hope that's all,' Rona said in concern. 'We don't want you coming down with anything.'

Fervently, Shan agreed but where Rona was worried about the film, she was anxious not to be confined to Faraway for any reason. She made an effort to look composed. 'I'm all right, really. Let's get this show on the road.'

Tammy emerged from the make-up van looking radiant in her Victorian wedding gown. It had been made to fit the actress originally cast in the role of Libby, but had needed little alteration to suit her slim figure. Her fine blonde hair had been threaded with ribbons and she looked the very picture of wedding-day innocence.

She was immediately surrounded by an admiring group of local people, many of whom thrust pieces of paper into her hands to be autographed. She obliged them with queenly grace.

'Looks like she's in her element,' sniffed Rona.

'She's entitled to enjoy her taste of stardom,' Shan said charitably. 'She's unlikely to get the same treatment in the larger acting world for some time yet.'

'Personal considerations aside, she really ought to try her luck in Sydney,' Rona said. 'She has a lot of talent.'

Shan agreed readily. 'I know. But I daren't suggest that because she already thinks I'm keen to get rid of her.'

'She's got to leave home sooner or later, surely?'

'I know.' What Rona didn't know was that when she did leave it would be on her own terms, knowing that her place at Faraway was being held open for her.

King's plan to set Dave up in his own production company had made sure of that.

Rona started towards the group surrounding Tammy, saying over her shoulder, 'I'll see if I can tear our star away from her fans.'

Slowly, Shan followed Rona to where Tammy was holding court. 'Sorry to break up the party kids, but we're losing light,' Rona said apologetically.

One by one, the teenagers moved back to an area set aside for observers, well out of camera range. A tall, willowy brunette with a fabulous suntan was the last to leave. She eyed Tammy a little wistfully. 'I sure wish I had your talent. I'd love to be a movie actress.'

'It's not as much fun as it looks, Helen,' Tammy told her friend with surprising honesty.

'Well anyway, good luck,' Helen said in parting.

As she passed Shan, she smiled warmly. 'I used to go to school with Tammy when we were a lot younger. You're the producer of this film, aren't you.'

Surprised to be recognised, Shan smiled back. 'That's right.'

Helen glanced back at Tammy. 'She sure is lucky to have a mother like you.'

At once, the familiar shuttered look came over Tammy and she tensed as if for flight. All traces of warmth towards her former school friend were erased. 'She isn't my mother,' came the chilly voice. 'I only have one mother and that was Joanna Price.'

Helen looked flustered. 'What did I say? I only meant . . .'

Murmuring sympathetically, Rona put an arm around the girl's shoulders and steered her towards the observers' area.

When they were out of earshot, Tammy fixed Shan with a malevolent glare. 'I suppose you put her up to saying that?'

Shan put a hand to her head which had begun to ache badly. 'Please, Tammy . . .'

'Not everyone thinks Shan comes a poor second to your precious mother,' defended Rona, coming up behind them.

Tammy opened her mouth to reply just as Dave's voice carried across the clearing. 'Ready on the set, Tammy.'

Her face set, Tammy flounced past them, pausing only to whisper to Shan, 'You'll regret that, I promise you.'

Rona watched her join Dave on the steps of the old homestead. 'Saved by the bell.'

'Thanks for coming to my rescue but it wasn't necessary. She doesn't mean half the things she says.'

Clucking her tongue impatiently, Rona folded her arms across her chest. 'When are you going to stop making excuses for that little minx?'

'You don't understand, she's had a pretty rough life.'

'There you go again! Lots of people come from broken homes—me for one. But we don't let it turn us into selfish monsters.'

Shan regarded Rona with astonishment. 'I didn't know your parents were divorced.'

'When I was eight. I spent term times with my mother and holidays with my father. But I don't see the need to wear the fact like a label.'

Maybe she had gone too far in making allowances for Tammy, Shan pondered. Having grown up in a happy, secure family of her own, she had assumed that anything less was bound to damage a child in some way. But Rona was one of the happiest, healthiest and best adjusted people she knew. However, unlike Tammy, Rona hadn't been the central figure in a custody dispute or lost her mother after the divorce.

'There I go again, making allowances,' she told herself. Still, it was a difficult habit to break.

'How does this look, Shan?' Dave called to her.

Shrugging off her personal worries, she stepped up to the camera and looked through the viewfinder. The wedding party was assembled on the front steps of the old homestead which had been dressed to look lived-in.

The actor playing the minister looked very convincing in his period suit and the boy playing the groom looked suitably uncomfortable in his wedding finery. Tammy held Jason's arm as the actor, playing her father, prepared to give her away in marriage.

The script called for Libby to keep darting nervous glances at the surrounding bush. She alone knew that her aboriginal suitor planned to rescue her from the arranged marriage.

The scene went like clockwork, with the tribesmen rushing in just before Libby could say 'I do'. As planned, the tribal elder knocked Jason to the ground and snatched Libby away.

Just when Shan thought they were going to do the scene in one take, Dave called 'Cut!'

She shot him a puzzled glance. 'What went wrong?'

'Jason was supposed to be unconscious but he moved.'

'It's this blasted dust, it got into my nose,' the actor complained.

Shan sighed. 'Let's do it again.'

The first take was apparently a fluke. Several tries later, they had still not achieved a flawless performance.

'What's the matter this time?' she asked Dave when he stopped the film yet again.

'Tammy, weren't you supposed to know about the raid?' he asked irritably.

'Of course,' she snapped back.

'Then why the dramatic screams when you were being taken away?'

'I was improvising,' she said archly.

He looked at her in disbelief. 'You were what?'

'It occurred to me during that last take that if Libby didn't put up some resistance, the others would know that she was in on the whole thing.'

Dave raked a hand through his hair, making it stand up in spikes which gave him an eccentric appearance.

'Careful, Tammy,' Shan thought, recognising the danger signs. So far, Tammy had only encountered the sweet lovable side of Dave's nature. She was still to come up against his other side, a demanding inflexibility where his work was concerned. It gave him a temper to match Tammy's worst outbursts.

'Well fancy that,' he said in a tone which dripped sarcasm. 'Little Tammy Falconer decided to rewrite the script in mid-scene. Pity she didn't tell the rest of us.'

There were some titters among the crew and Tammy's face reddened, but it was soon clear that she was blushing from annoyance rather than embarassment. 'It's an actor's job to interpret the script as she sees fit,' she defended herself.

'It's an actor's job to do as she's told,' Dave responded. 'Now for God's sake let's get this scene in the can—and without the histrionics this time, Miss Falconer.'

The others returned to their marks but Tammy stayed where she was, her expression defiant. 'Not until you agree to do the scene my way.'

Dave's thunderous expression should have been warning enough, but he added, 'We'll do the scene the way it was written. There *are* other actresses, you know.'

Shan caught at his arm. 'Dave, please . . .'

'Stay out of this, Shan. I know you're on Tammy's side but it's time somebody pointed out to her that she doesn't run the world.'

'But I do say what happens on this picture,' Tammy interjected. 'My father is backing it.'

This was the moment Shan had dreaded. Tammy had never been afraid of using any power she possessed, and the fact that King was funding the film gave her a tailor-made weapon. 'We'll have to let her do it her way,' she told Dave in an undertone.

'No. If I give in now, she'll be running the show from here on and that isn't fair to you or any of us on the project.'

'I know, but . . .'

'Well? Have you decided?' Tammy asked imperiously, plainly irked by the whispered discussion between Dave and Shan.

Dave gave Shan an apologetic look. 'You aren't running this operation, Tammy, nor is the backer—whoever he happens to be. So we do the scene the way it's written—or not at all. It's up to you. We'll take a lunch break to give you time to think about it.'

Without a backward look he strode away towards the shelter of the camera truck and stood pensively in the shade.

Shan joined him there. 'I hope we're doing the right thing.'

'I hope so too,' he said in a low voice. 'But we can't let her think she can run the show, no matter who she is.' He gave Shan a compassionate glance. 'I'm sorry if my strategy backfires, Shan. It could mean the end of the film but I hope you understand why I'm doing it?'

'Of course, and I'm with you all the way.' Whether he knew it or not, Dave was fighting for his independence as a man, as well as a professional. Tammy had counted on his being in love with her to give her power over him, but he dared not let her rule him now or there was no future for them as a couple.

Shan recognised the power struggle they were engaged in. She had fought the same battle for independence with King during their marriage when she refused to submerge her needs in Tammy's problems. She could have stayed married to King if she had allowed Tammy to ride roughshod over her, but she had asserted herself and lost. She hoped Dave would fare better than she had—for all their sakes.

John and Rona joined them in the patch of shade. 'Not eating?' Shan asked.

'Too tense. Do you think she'll give in?'

'How do I know, Rona?' Dave said. 'I only know this confrontation is overdue. She's been testing me for days now.'

John drew his gaze back from the surrounding hills. 'What does this business remind you of?'

Shan shook her head. 'You tell us.'

'The old days when we worked with Tammy's mother. Joanna Price used to make every film into a pitched battle between the producers and herself. She always knew what was best for the film—which was usually what best for Joanna Price.'

There was a shriek of dismay from the end of the truck where Tammy had apparently been eavesdropping. 'You're all horrible,' she seethed. 'You're picking on me just to get even with my mother because she was so much better than the rest of you— why don't you admit it?'

'It's nothing like that, Tammy,' Shan intervened.

The teenager rounded on her. 'As for you, you've been jealous of her success all along.'

'That's not true!' Shan gasped, feeling her face drain of colour.

'Then why else do you keep saying terrible things

about her. I'm her daughter, I should know what she was like and you're not worthy to live in the same house, far less sleep in her bed with her husband.'

Shocked beyond words, Shan felt the sting of tears behind her eyes and fought for self-control. But before she could say anything, John stepped forward. 'I've heard about enough. The other day I regretted being honest about your mother, now I'm sorry I didn't say more. I worked with this paragon whom you so admire and I tell you, Shan is worth ten of her for integrity and guts.'

'John, don't,' begged Shan.

But having started, he was determined to say his piece. 'If she intends to work in this business, she'd better get used to hearing the truth,' he said angrily. 'Joanna Price was . . .'

'That's enough!' came a commanding voice which cracked like a whiplash, silencing them all. Shan hadn't noticed King returning, being too intent on the drama taking place beside the truck. She winced as he strode towards them. 'What the hell's going on here?'

'They're all being horrible to me,' whimpered Tammy.

King gave her a withering look then turned to Dave. 'I was asking you, Cameron.'

Dave launched into a summary of what had taken place. King heard him out in grim silence then turned to Tammy. 'Is this true?'

In the face of his forbidding appraisal, she quailed. 'Well I did think since it was your film, I had some rights.'

'I wasn't aware that it was my film. I thought it was a Penrose Production.'

Shan started. She couldn't believe her ears. He was actually defending her! Her pleasure was short-lived however. 'I'd like to have a talk with you,' he said curtly, before turning back to Tammy. 'If you're going to make a career of this you'd better start learning how to be part of a team. Now go and finish the scene the way you should have done it in the first place.'

It was a very chastened Tammy who took her place on the set with the rest of the cast. This time the scene progressed without a hitch. 'That's a take,' Dave announced at last and everyone relaxed.

Only Shan remained tense, aware that King still had something to say to her. Publicly, he had taken her side against Tammy but privately, she didn't know what to expect. 'I'll drive you back,' he said in a tone which brooked no argument.

In the car, she waited for him to speak first. After several miles passed in stony silence, she could stand it no longer. 'Why don't you say it?'

'Say what?'

'That I put John up to criticising Joanna again. It is what you're thinking, isn't it?'

He sighed heavily. 'I don't know what to think any more. Tammy's my only child. Maybe I haven't been as objective about her as I should have been.'

She stared at him in amazement. 'You mean you don't blame me for what happened today?'

'I blame myself, mostly. It never entered my head that she would try to blackmail you into doing things her way just because I was funding the picture.'

It was what Joanna would have done, Shan reflected but bit back the observation. 'She's very young,' she said instead.

'Youth doesn't excuse everything. Hell, Shan, maybe I have been short-sighted about this. I've always thought of Tammy as an innocent but somewhere along the line, she grew up and I didn't notice.'

'It happens to us all,' she said sardonically. Right now, she felt a million years old herself.

He gave her a sideways glance filled with compassion. 'This has really been rough on you, hasn't it?'

She blinked away tears which threatened to spill over at any time. She could take almost anything but his pity. 'For goodness sake, say what you want to say,' she ground out.

His knuckles whitened as he gripped the steering wheel. 'What I'm trying to say is that maybe you're right. Maybe we aren't good for one another.'

She looked at him, dumb-founded. 'I don't understand?'

'I'm giving you your freedom, damn it! The divorce you wanted and whatever cash settlement you need to make a new life for yourself. I'm getting out of your life, Shan, isn't that what you wanted?'

Suddenly she felt bereft, like a piece of flotsam washed up on a deserted shore. 'I suppose so,' she said in a low tone. 'But I don't want your money. I can manage well enough on what I make in my work.'

'So you won't even let me help you financially? I didn't realise you hated me that much.'

Hated him? Dear God, if he only knew! But he still hadn't mentioned telling Tammy the truth about her mother, the one thing which would give them a chance. Instead, he had taken her at her word and was releasing her from their marriage.

She had achieved what she wanted. So why did she feel as if her world had come to an end?

CHAPTER NINE

NEXT morning, even the sun streaming through her bedroom window couldn't lift Shan's spirits. As soon as she opened her eyes she knew what was wrong. King had agreed to let her go.

She should have been pleased that the years of uncertainty would soon be over but all she felt was a sense of failure.

There was a tap on her door then she heard Mrs Gordon's exaggerated whisper. 'Are you awake?'

'Yes, Mrs G. You can come in.'

Mrs Gordon pushed open the door, juggling a tea tray in one hand. 'I thought you'd like an early morning cuppa.'

'That was kind of you but you shouldn't go to so much trouble.'

The housekeeper smiled. 'It's no trouble at all dear. You haven't been looking too well lately so I thought a bit of pampering wouldn't hurt.'

To please her, Shan took a sip of the steaming tea. Satisfied, Mrs Gordon retreated, saying, 'I'll see you at breakfast.'

As soon as she had gone, Shan set the cup down and bolted for the bathroom where she was wretchedly ill. It was the third time in a row that she had awoken feeling like this. Rona must be right. She was coming down with something.

The sight of her white face staring back at her from the mirror gave her a jolt. What if she was ... oh no! Surely she couldn't be pregnant after just one night with King?

Shakily, she returned to the bedroom and checked the dates in her diary. They tallied. Added to the bouts of morning sickness and the unaccustomed tiredness she'd been feeling lately, it seemed likely.

What was she going to do? If she told King she was expecting his baby, there was no way he would agree to let her go—far less to give her a divorce. She knew only too well how possessive he could be and he was quite capable of expecting her to sacrifice her own happiness so he could have his child.

It was her child, too. He didn't want her any more, making all his plans around Tammy and Dave. So why shouldn't she make her own plans for the baby and herself? He need never know of the child's existence.

The idea began to take root and she felt a sense of rising excitement. She would have to give up her production company of course, the income being too precarious now. But she would be welcome on the payroll of most big production houses, so she should have no trouble supporting the two of them. She might have to accept some cash from King after all, to carry her through until the baby was born. He would think it odd that she had changed her mind, but she was sure he wouldn't deny her the assistance. She could always repay him once she was earning again.

The two of us. The idea brought with it a wave of tenderness only tinged by sadness that the baby would never know his . . . or her . . . father. At least when she could no longer have King, she would have his child as a living, breathing part of him for the rest of her life. Tammy could never take that away from her.

The dining room was deserted when she went in to breakfast. As she hesitated at the table, Mrs Gordon brought in a large jug of fresh orange juice.

'Where is everybody?' she asked.

'Mr Falconer and Tammy are shut up in the study having a talk,' the housekeeper told her conspiratorially. 'I don't know what's up, but it looks serious.'

Not wanting to encourage gossip, Shan made no comment as the housekeeper filled her glass with juice. 'What else can I get you?' she asked. 'Eggs, bacon?'

The very thought of fried food made Shan feel nauseous so she shook her head. 'Just some toast, thank you.'

Mrs Gordon gave her a penetrating look. 'Nothing the matter is there?'

Shan made an effort to brighten. 'No, everything's fine. I think I've been working too hard.'

Shaking her head in disapproval, Mrs Gordon went off to the kitchen to fetch the toast.

Soon afterwards, a very subdued-looking Tammy came into the dining room and flung herself into a chair without so much as a 'good morning' for Shan.

'Is anything wrong?' she asked tentatively.

Tammy gave her a malevolent look and tossed her blonde hair expressively. 'You just can't stay out of my life, can you?'

'I only asked whether anything was wrong?' Shan said, baffled. She was used to animosity from Tammy but hostility with no cause was something new.

'That wasn't what I meant as well you know,' Tammy said sullenly. She seemed about to add something more when King walked into the room.

At once, the teenager scraped her chair back and fled from the room.

'Good morning, Shan,' he said coolly, apparently unmoved by Tammy's display of temper. Although he acted unconcerned towards Shan, the shadows in his eyes betrayed him. Since their talk last night, the lines etched down the sides of his mouth had deepened and his skin had lost some of its golden sheen. When he spoke to Shan he avoided meeting her eyes. In spite of herself, she felt a surge of compassion towards him. However much divided them, he was still her husband and very likely the father of her child.

She looked uncertainly after Tammy. 'What was that all about?'

He quirked an eyebrow upwards. 'Nothing that need concern you.'

'Tammy seems to think it does. What did you say to her to get her so upset?'

He poured coffee for himself before he answered. 'As I told you yesterday, I didn't realise how spoiled Tammy had become. So I took your advice. This morning I asked her how serious she was about becoming an actress. When she assured me she intended to reach the top, I gave her the option of going to Sydney to undertake professional training or giving it up altogether. Not surprisingly, she agreed to try her wings away from home although she made it clear she was only agreeing under duress. Still, I'm sure it will do her more good than harm.'

So that was why Tammy had been so hostile. 'I agree she has a future as an actress if she applies herself but it was a pity you told her it was my idea. Now she'll think it's another ploy of mine to get rid of her.'

'Under the circumstances, it doesn't matter any more, does it?'

She knew he was referring to their talk last night. Since they were dissolving their marriage, it no longer mattered what Tammy thought of her. The awareness only added fuel to her growing unhappiness.

Just then, Mrs Gordon came in with a lavish cooked breakfast for King and a plate of toast for Shan. The sight of the hot food nearly made her ill again but she fought down the sensation, averting her eyes from the plate. To try to settle her rebellious stomach, she ate a few bites of the dry toast.

King looked at her meagre meal with distaste. 'Surely you aren't dieting, Shan? I would have thought that overweight was the last of your worries.'

'Looks are important when you're a single woman,' she said and saw an expression of pain darken his eyes. She hardened her heart. This course was his choice, not hers.

He set his knife and fork down. 'Shan, it doesn't have to be like this you know.'

'Yes it does. You said yourself that we aren't good for each other. Which reminds me . . .'

'Yes?'

Nervously, she drew a pattern on the tablecloth with her finger, bending her head to avoid meeting his eyes. 'You mentioned a cash settlement. I . . . I've changed my mind about accepting your help.'

His expression grew stony. She could almost hear what he was thinking: so greed finally overcame her pride. Well he could think what he liked. She had her baby to consider and if she had to sacrifice a little pride for her child's wellbeing, it was probably only the first of many sacrifices she would be called upon to make.

'Just work out how much you'll need and I'll have the money transferred to your account in Sydney,' he said flatly.

She longed to tell him what the money would be used for, hating to have him think she wanted it for her own pleasure. But knowing how he would respond if he knew about the baby gave her the strength to keep silent. 'Thank you,' she said instead.

They finished their meal in chilly silence, each preoccupied with their own thoughts. Foremost in

Shan's mind was the need to confirm her pregnancy as soon as possible. She would have to ask the unit's medical officer to check her over. Knowing how quickly gossip travelled in the film world, she would have to rely on the doctor's discretion. King mustn't find out about the baby before she could leave Faraway.

Draining her coffee cup, she stood up. 'I'd better get to work.'

To her surprise, he placed a hand on her arm. 'Don't go just yet, please. We haven't had a proper talk since you got here.'

She was sorely tempted to sit down again and pour out her heart to him, but what was the point? She had done everything she could to get along with Tammy and been rejected. Now King had rejected her too. She couldn't take any more of this emotional tug-of-war, especially not with the likelihood that a baby was involved.

'I can't stay. I have a team of stunt men flying up from Melbourne for the buffalo scene. At their rates of pay, I can't afford to keep them waiting around.'

A shadow passed across his face. 'I see. Your work must come first, of course.'

'You're wrong,' she said quietly. 'There was a time when I willingly put my work aside for you.'

'But not any more?'

'No, not this time.'

Heavy hearted, she left him sitting at the dining table and made her way upstairs to get ready for the day's filming. It was just as well that the film would be finished before her pregnancy really started to affect her. If her instincts proved her right, in a few weeks' time, she wouldn't be in any shape to handle a physically demanding day like the one which lay ahead.

In Joanna's bedroom—somehow, she still couldn't think of this Hollywood extravagance as her room— she changed into her oldest denim jeans and a bright red long-sleeved shirt which would protect her arms from the burning sun. She had already acquired a golden tan during her days here but didn't want to risk sunburn—not now. A broad brimmed bushman's hat was the final touch and she was ready for the day.

She met Dave outside the homestead. He was similarly dressed in working clothes. 'Have the stunt men arrived?' she asked.

'They're already pacing out the location,' he told her. 'The action co-ordinator is a bit worried about using wild buffaloes for the stampede sequence.'

'Didn't you tell him that the animals come from a wildlife park?'

Dave grinned. 'He says he doesn't believe there's such a thing as a tame buffalo.'

Remembering the lumbering beasts she had seen being rounded up by King's stockmen, she had a moment of doubt herself but recalled King saying the animals could be tamed after a week or so in a yard around men and horses. All you needed was a pen strong enough to hold them during their first days of captivity. She said as much to Dave. 'Tell that to the stunt men,' was all he said.

When she started to walk away he said, 'Aren't you coming with me?'

'No, I have something to do first. I'll join you later.'

'See you at the location then.'

As soon as he drove off she headed for the small dispensary which the unit's doctor, Mick Spalding, had taken over as his headquarters. So far there had been little call for his services but his presence was a wise precaution in country where the nearest medical help was the Flying Doctor Service which had to be summoned by radio.

The doctor looked surprised to see her. 'What can I do for you, Shan?'

He was even more surprised when she requested a pregnancy test but acceded readily. 'How soon will you have the results?' she asked afterwards.

'I can come out to the location with the news as soon as I've done the test,' he told her. 'I have to be there anyway. The stunt people want me on standby in case anything goes wrong.'

'I'd appreciate it,' she said.

'I suppose if there is a baby on the way, you'll go back to being Mrs Falconer again?'

Her eyes clouded and she said sadly, 'You suppose wrong. If I am pregnant, I don't want anyone to know about it, especially not King.'

Dr Spalding frowned. 'I must respect your wishes of course, but . . .'

'Thank you, that's all I ask,' she finished before he could say anything more.

She went straight from the doctor's office to the location where the stunt co-ordinator, Digger Matheson, was waiting for her.

When she first set eyes on him, she had trouble believing that such a rugged looking man could be afraid of anything. He was to double for Jason Cody in the scene where the actor was supposed to be tracking his daughter and her aboriginal suitor through the bush. The close-ups would be of Jason himself, but the long shots where the rider was engulfed in a buffalo stampede would be of Matheson.

'How many animals will we be using?' he asked Shan.

'Only four—a bull and some cows we've borrowed from a wildlife park.'

'Four buffaloes for a stampede?' He rolled his eyes expressively.

'Don't worry. The footage we take today will be intercut with library shots of a real stampede. It's not ideal, I know.'

'If you were Spielberg or Coppola, you'd have the real thing,' Digger told her.

'If I were Spielberg or Coppola, I could afford it,' she rejoined.

Grinning, he returned to his team as they marked out the route of the 'stampede'. Although everything would appear to happen chaotically, in fact each step of the action was painstakingly choreographed in advance.

They rigged up tripwires and small explosions which would churn up the dust when a rider and his horse fell under the buffaloes' hooves. Where necessary, the overhanging tree branches were pruned back to ensure they wouldn't behead a charging rider.

Outside the make-up van, Jason and Tammy were in consultation with one of the stunt men. Jason was dressed exactly the same as Digger in riding moleskins, checked shirts and broad brimmed hats. Digger's hairline had been changed by make-up so it matched Jason's. To the audience, it would be impossible to tell whether scenes featured Jason or Digger.

As Shan watched, Tammy broke away and came over to her. She seemed to have recovered from her sulking fit of the morning and was smiling sweetly. 'Ah, there you are, Shan. How is everything?'

Surprised, but relieved at the girl's change of heart, Shan smiled back. 'So far so good. Has Digger briefed you on this scene?'

'Every inch of the way. My job is mainly to scream a lot and stay out of the way of the animals.'

Shan couldn't resist making a comment. 'I'm glad you're in such good spirits now,' she said pointedly.

The teenager blushed prettily. 'If you're referring to this morning, I've had a chance to think about things. Going to Sydney won't be so bad. At least I can do Dad proud since he'll be backing my films.'

'Of course. He's going into the production business, I believe.'

'Only as a backer. Once Dave and I are married, he's going to set Dave up in his own studio. He won't have to look far for his leading lady.'

'I'm very glad for both of you,' Shan said bleakly. Tammy's happiness only served to remind her of how empty her own future was going to be once she returned to Sydney. But she would have the baby, she told herself determinedly. Apart from the physical signs, she had a growing certainty that she was pregnant. No amount of medical confirmation could be stronger than the awareness she sensed of life quickening inside her. She smiled contentedly.

'You look very pleased with yourself,' Tammy said sharply, bringing Shan back to the present.

'Shouldn't I?'

Tammy relaxed visibly, aware that her tone had sharpened. 'Of course you should, since the film is going so well. There's only one thing . . .'

'What's that?'

'I hesitate to ask, since you and I haven't been getting along so well but . . .'

'Go ahead, I won't bite,' Shan urged impatiently.

'Before we start filming, I wonder if I could take a picture of you for my album.'

This time, Shan couldn't keep the surprise out of her voice. 'You want a photograph of me?'

Tammy's expression became engaging. 'I have so few family album pictures. Most of those I have of mother are professional studio shots. And Dad would much rather be behind a camera than in front of one. Please say yes?'

Compassion overcame suspicion in Shan's mind. What harm could posing for a snapshot do? It was the first time Tammy had ever asked her for anything, and it was ironic that she chose the very time when Shan and King had decided to go their separate ways. 'Oh very well,' she conceded. 'But we'd better not take too long. The others will be waiting for us.'

Tammy dismissed the others with an airy wave of her hand. 'According to Digger, they'll be another hour setting up the stunts so there's no rush.'

'Where did you want to take the picture?'

'What about against the backdrop of the lagoon?'

Shan looked around. The lagoon did indeed look picturesque although it was probably a familiar sight to Tammy, who had grown up amid such beauty.

Beyond the thicket of pandanus palms, a mob of Big Red kangaroos cropped the grass, ignoring the film people, while giant jabirus and smaller cranes fished the shallows for food. Overhead, a flock of hoarsely chuckling corellas flew from tree to tree.

Shan walked to the water's edge, this time casting a wary eye out for crocodiles, not wanting to repeat her previous performance when one had been allowed to sneak up on her. Underfoot, the brittle carpet of sun-dried leaves crackled like gunshots. 'Will this do?' she asked, posing side-on at the water's edge.

Tammy reached for a camera lying on the bonnet of a Land Rover. Busily, she focused on Shan and set dials and switches. 'Great!' she said at last. 'Say cheese.'

'Cheese,' said Shan obligingly. She hoped her Mona Lisa half-smile was adequate because she didn't feel in the mood for anything sunnier, despite Tammy's apparent change of heart towards her. What had brought it about? she wondered.

She heard the click of the camera and relaxed, starting back towards the tennager. 'Is that it?'

'Just one more please—with a different backdrop this time?'

'All right,' she said resignedly. 'Where would you like me to stand this time?'

Tammy thought for a moment. 'What about a souvenir of this picture? I'd like to have something to remember the film by, then when I'm rich and famous, I'll look back fondly on my first major role.'

All this sounded too ingenuous for Shan's liking but she couldn't put a finger on exactly what was amiss. She only knew that alarm bells were sounding in her head. 'How about we take one alongside the make-up van?' she proposed. 'It has the company name and the film title on the side?'

'No, too cliché,' Tammy objected, then brightened. 'I know. What about one of you on the rail of the buffalo pen?'

Shan looked warily at the massive yard King's team had erected for the buffaloes which were being used in the stampede scene. It looked strong enough to hold the huge beasts but ... 'I don't know,' she wavered.

'Please? Just one shot.'

She decided to get this over with. Whatever Tammy was up to, she would have to reveal it soon or they would start filming. Besides, the yard was very substantial and she had seen the wild animals charging posts and rails like these, out on the plains. Even the largest and wildest bulls hadn't been able to budge them.

Putting her trust in King's handiwork, she vaulted up on to the railing which was made from old railway sleepers. She cursed as a splinter scored her hand. The topmost rail was seven feet from the ground and reaching it, she clung to it tightly as she looked down at the yarded animals.

They seemed harmless enough and regarded her with large, luminous eyes. Of course they were used to humans, being on constant display in a wildlife park, she reminded herself. Still, the sight of the bull's long thick horns, standing straight out on each side of its massive head, made her shudder inwardly. Tame or not, she wouldn't care to be any closer to it than she was now.

'Have you taken the picture yet?' she called down nervously to Tammy.

The girl was fiddling with her camera. 'Just a minute. The autofocus is stuck. I'll have to set it manually.'

'Well hurry will you.' Below her, the bull sniffed at the air, catching her scent. His feet shuffled uneasily and he inched closer.

'I suppose you're happy that I'm going to Sydney,' Tammy said chattily as she fiddled with the camera.

Shan kept a wary eye on the animals below her. 'Why should I be?'

'Wasn't that what you wanted—to have Dad and Faraway all to yourself?'

So King hadn't told her that Shan was leaving too. 'It really won't make any difference,' she said. 'Since I won't be here either. Your father and I have agreed that we aren't suited to one another.'

Tammy looked at her in consternation. 'So you had nothing to do with Dad sending me away?'

'I told him your career would benefit from the experience,' Shan admitted. 'But the rest was his own idea.'

Under her film make-up, Tammy's face had drained of colour. 'I didn't know, Shan,' she whispered. 'For God's sake get down from there!'

'What's the matter?' Shan asked uneasily.

Her stepdaughter's voice rose to a scream. 'Just get down, quickly.'

As Shan started to clamber down from the railing, the bull charged, thundering against the massive posts with an impact which made the ground tremble. Shan screamed but held her grip on the railing, feeling the rough timber tear at the tender skin of her palms. Again, the great beast threw himself at the railing but this time she was able to jump clear before he crashed against it. She landed on the ground shaken but unhurt, nursing her torn hands.

Dave came rushing up to her. 'My God, Shan, are you all right? What were you doing up there?'

She darted a glance at Tammy who stood there shaking. 'I was posing for a snapshot.'

'A snapshot? You could have been killed.'

'But I thought these were tame animals.'

'They are, to a degree. But that big bull has an unfortunate history. When he was a calf, some hooligans broke into the wildlife park and threw firebombs at him from a tree. He's tame enough when people are on his level but he gets nervous of anyone looming above his head. I was warned about it when he was brought here. Apparently the story is quite common knowledge in these parts. He's a bit of a bovine celebrity.'

He followed her glance to where Tammy stood. 'Surely you knew about it, Tammy?'

'No, she . . . she couldn't have,' Shan said aghast. Even her stepdaughter wouldn't be so callous as to expose her to such danger. 'It was an accident so let's leave it at that. Luckily I'm not hurt, just a bit shaken up. Let's all get back to work.'

As the others walked away, she saw Tammy reach for Dave's arm but he shrugged her off and kept walking. Tammy followed in his wake but Shan couldn't hear what she was saying.

She spun around as Dr Spalding came up to her, looking worried. 'You'll have to take better care of yourself than that now,' he said seriously.

A thrill of excitement gripped her, eclipsing the shock. 'You mean . . .'

'No doubt about it. But don't worry, it's a normal pregnancy so far. I'll give you a note for your doctor in Sydney and if you come and see me at the end of the day, I'll brief you on what you should be doing in the meantime.'

Anxiously, she looked around but no one else was within earshot. 'You will keep this to yourself, won't you?' she asked.

'You have my word. But don't you think the father deserves to be told?'

For all that he fitted in well with the exotic world of film-making, Mick Spalding was an old-fashioned doctor who believed in the sanctity of the family. He would keep nagging her until she gave in and allowed him to tell King the truth. There was only one way she could think of to dissuade him. 'You're right,' she said softly, lowering her head. 'But that would depend on who the father was, wouldn't it?'

She lifted her head to find him regarding her with sorrowful understanding. 'I see. Somehow I didn't think that was your way, Shan.'

She hated herself for misleading him, even though she hadn't told him an outright lie. 'So you see why King can't be told?' she said earnestly.

He nodded. 'Yes, of course. It would have been a terrible blunder under the circumstances. I assume you do want the baby? You won't do anything silly?'

As if she would consider such a thing! 'I want this

baby more than anything else in the world,' she said fervently.

Some of the uneasiness left his face. 'That's something at least.' Gently he turned her palms upwards and tut-tutted at the abrasions on them. 'Stay here while I get you something to put on those. You have had your tetanus innoculations, I hope.'

'Yes, I had a booster as a precaution before I left Sydney,' she confirmed, relieved to be off the topic of her pregnancy. He headed in the direction of his car and while she waited, she turned her attention to the stunt men.

They had nearly finished setting up the shot and Digger was walking the horses through the scene while King's stockmen rode along the sidelines. Soon it would be time for Dave to clear the set and release the buffaloes. The shot would have to be obtained in one take as the animals would be too skittish afterwards, to risk a retake. As it was, it would take King's team some time to round the buffaloes up after they were turned loose. Although they had been raised in captivity, they would still be attracted by the scent of freedom.

Her own encounter with the bull made her shudder. She still couldn't believe that Tammy would deliberately send her up on to the railing, knowing the bull's reputation. And yet Tammy was the one who suggested the climb, only changing her mind when she found out that Shan wasn't responsible for her being sent away.

To take her mind off her close call she made herself think about the baby. Her baby. Or more accurately, hers and King's. For despite what she had allowed the doctor to think, there was no question of any other man being the father. Having his child would be like having a part of him to keep forever. It was the one thing which made the prospect of leaving Faraway bearable.

Bag in hand, the doctor started back towards her. Then she heard a frantic shout behind her. 'Shan, look out!'

The bull's repeated charges must have loosened the fastening of the buffalo pen. As she spun around, she was horrified to see the gate standing open and the bull bearing down on her, his nostrils flaring.

As he homed in on the scarlet splash of her shirt, she knew she should find a tree to climb to escape those lethal horns. During her previous stay at Faraway King had drummed this basic survival tactic into her. But now that the danger was imminent, she was literally rooted to the spot. Try as she might to will her legs to move, they refused to obey her.

Everything happened too fast for conscious thought after that. The ground beneath her shook with the onrush of the great animal and she was riveted by the sight of its huge spread of horns. Then the breath was knocked from her body as she was sent spinning sideways by an unknown hand. She was buffeted by the leathery texture of the slate-grey hide as the bull rushed past her, but the horns missed her altogether.

With the skill born of long experience, the mounted stockmen moved to either side of the runaway bull, steering him away from the crew. He had apparently decided he had had enough of humans for one day and bolted for the bush without a backward glance.

Thrown hard against the dusty ground, Shan felt the universe growing darker. Blood roared in her ears and she sagged against the unyielding earth, blind and paralysed.

Dave's voice came as if from a great distance. 'Shan, are you all right? For God's sake answer me?'

She tried desperately to tell him that she was

conscious but her senses refused to co-operate. She could hear their voices but could see and feel nothing. It was as if she was in a pitch dark room listening to them over an intercom.

First there was Dave's voice, high-pitched with worry over her. 'Doctor, get over here quickly. I think she's paralysed.'

Then came Dr Spalding's more controlled response. 'Everybody move back and let me take a look at her.'

If the doctor examined her then, she had no awareness of it. Because at that point, her hearing deserted her too, and for a long time afterwards, she knew nothing.

CHAPTER TEN

THE hands which smoothed the damp hair back from her forehead were cool and gentle. She shifted slightly and groaned at the pain the movement cost her, retreating instinctively into the cocoon of non-existence where pain was only a memory.

Some time later—hours or days, she couldn't be sure—the same hands arranged the bedclothes more comfortably around her and smoothed away the creases from her pillow. This time, movement was not quite so painful but she was still reluctant to leave her cocoon. 'King?' she murmured aloud.

'I'm here, my darling.' Did she imagine it or did his lips brush her mouth with infinite tenderness?

There was something she knew she should ask him, something important. But what was it? Then she had it. 'My baby? Is my baby all right?'

'Sssh. The doctor says your baby is all right,' King assured her. 'Rest now. Sleep.'

Secure in the knowledge that the life within her was safe, she drifted off into oblivion again, unaware of the blissful smile which played around her lips.

When next she awoke, it was to full consciousness, to find Dr Spalding bending over her. She must have imagined that King was here those other times.

'What happened?' she murmured drowsily.

The doctor smiled. 'The sleeping beauty awakens at last. Don't you remember being knocked over by the buffalo?'

A thrill of fear coursed through her. 'Yes, I remember now. Someone pushed me out of its path but I don't know who.'

'Luckily King could see what was happening and rode in at full gallop, distracting the buffalo. In any case, I'm told it was only trying to escape, not to harm you.'

A glint of amusement sparkled in her eyes. 'Now you tell me.' She flexed her limbs experimentally. 'Am I all right?'

'Apart from assorted bruises and the concussion which put you out for a couple of days, you'll be fine, thanks to King. The buffalo only caught you a glancing blow.'

She shuddered at the recollection, then her eyes grew wide. 'Doctor, what about the baby?'

He patted her shoulder reassuringly. 'Your baby's all right, by a miracle. I'll arrange for you to have some tests when you get back to Sydney, just to be certain, but I don't think there's anything to worry about.'

She subsided against the pillows, relief bringing tears to her eyes. 'Thank goodness. I was so frightened.'

'Well you can relax. You need all the rest you can get from now on—even without getting in the way of charging buffaloes.'

She grimaced. 'Believe me, it wasn't my idea. By the way, have you been with me all the time?'

The doctor looked uncomfortable. 'No. As a matter of fact, your husband sat with you most of the time. He wouldn't let anyone else take over.'

In growing horror, she remembered the things she had said while she was semi-conscious. She had asked King, of all people, about the baby. 'So he knows,' she said dully.

'You told him yourself. Afterwards, he came and asked me if it was true.'

'And you told him everything?'

'Only what you told me. At first he was convinced that he must be the father, but I didn't think it was fair to let him go on thinking the wrong thing.'

She could hardly force her lips to frame the question. 'How did he take it?'

'I don't know. He drove out of here like a maniac before I had a chance to ask him.'

Tears of anguish flooded her eyes and she turned her head into the pillow. 'Oh my God!'

Dr Spalding moved closer and tilted her face to look at him. 'You mean he *is* your baby's father?'

She nodded dumbly, biting her lower lip. 'I said what I did so you wouldn't talk me into telling him. I was afraid he would pressure me into staying if he found out. There hasn't been anyone else.'

'Oh, Shan, I'm so sorry.'

'No, it isn't your fault. You did what you thought was best. I shouldn't have tried to deceive you.'

He eased his shoulders back and only then, she noticed the lines of fatigue in his face. 'It's done now. Is there anything I can do to make amends?'

She shook her head. 'There's nothing anyone can do now.'

'Poor Shan. You'd better try and get some rest if you can.'

If she could. It seemed a forlorn hope. After the doctor left she tossed and turned in the bed ignoring the pain of her healing bruises. So King believed that she was pregnant by another man. What must he think of her?

Not that it mattered now, she thought miserably. He had already decided it was best if they went their separate ways so this would only convince him he had made the right decision. The fact that he had driven off as soon as he received the news from Dr Spalding must mean that he didn't want to see her again.

If that was true, why had he insisted on sitting with her until she began to recover? Of course, he hadn't known about the baby then.

'Damn, damn, damn,' she said over and over into the pillow. It felt damp and she realised that she had allowed a few tears to fall after promising herself she wouldn't give in to them. She had to be strong now, for her child's sake if not for her own.

'Not tears, surely?' said a motherly voice. She looked up as Mrs Gordon came into the room bearing a laden tray.

She gulped back her tears. 'It seems to be your lot in life to bring me meals in bed.'

Mrs Gordon beamed. 'That's better. I do seem to be making a habit of it, don't I? Still, I don't mind. The doctor said you should try to eat something to build up your strength.'

She uncovered the tray and showed Shan the chicken broth and buttered toast she had brought. 'Just eat what you can and leave the rest.'

'Thanks, I will,' Shan assured her.

She propped herself upright against the pillows and the housekeeper placed the tray across her knees. 'Would you like me to feed you?'

'Goodness, no. I can manage thanks.' She took a spoonful of the soup and to her surprise, found she was ravenous. Enthusiastically, she began to eat.

Watching her with satisfaction, Mrs Gordon made herself comfortable on the foot of the bed. 'That's the girl. I made it for you myself. Mr Falconer always enjoys my home-made chicken soup and I knew you wouldn't want anything heavier yet.'

'No this is fine. Delicious in fact.' She wished Mrs Gordon hadn't mentioned King. The thought that he was unable to face her took the edge off her appetite.

But Mrs Gordon seemed inclined to say more and with her mouth full, Shan couldn't do anything to dissuade her. 'You know that young Tammy ran away after your accident?'

Shan's spoon froze in mid-air. 'She what?'

'She took off during all the fuss. She had the crazy idea that the accident was somehow her fault.'

'Where on earth would she get a notion like that?'

Mrs Gordon shrugged. 'Who knows? You know what she's like when she gets a bee in her bonnet about something. But Mr Falconer will soon make her see sense.'

'He's gone after her?' Shan asked.

'As soon as he knew you were all right. Not that I approve of him leaving you. His place is at your side, not chasing after a girl who should have more sense.'

'But she is his daughter,' Shan sighed. In any contest for King's attention, Tammy would always come out ahead of Shan. She had faced that fact long ago. Dispiritedly, she pushed the half-finished bowl of soup away. 'I can't eat any more.'

'Some of the toast then?' Mrs Gordon coaxed.

'No, really. I think I'd like to sleep a little if you don't mind.'

The housekeeper looked disappointed. She had apparently been hoping for a cosy chat while King and Tammy were away. Shan felt sorry for Mrs Gordon who meant no harm, but she wasn't up to talking about King yet, maybe never.

When the housekeeper had gone, she rolled over on her side and cradled her head on her arm. So Tammy believed that the accident was her fault. How could she havw arrived at such a conclusion? Unless . . .

Reluctantly Shan recalled how her stepdaughter had encouraged her to climb the rails of the buffalo pen, knowing that the bull had a fear of anyone looking down on him. If the animal hadn't been provoked into charging, the gate would have held securely. So in a way, Tammy *was* to blame, although surely she couldn't have meant any real harm to come to Shan?

She was making excuses for the girl again, she knew, but it seemed inconceivable that Tammy should hate her so much. She would probably have reacted just as strongly to anyone who tried to take her mother's place. Still, she couldn't suppress a shudder of horror as she thought about what might have happened if King hadn't intervened.

She must have slept for some time then, despite her mental turmoil, because the next thing she knew it was late afternoon and the room was shadowed. There was a gentle tap on the door then Rona's head appeared around it.

'Good, you're awake,' she said, coming in. 'How do you feel?'

'Like I've been run over by a charging buffalo,' Shan said listlessly.

Rona studied her in concern. 'Mick Spalding told me you were on the mend but you don't sound much like it.'

'I'm all right, really,' Shan assured her, not wanting to alarm her friend. Besides, her injuries were more of the spirit than the body now, and Mick Spalding couldn't do much about those. She patted the side of the bed. 'Sit down and tell me what's been happening with the film in the last couple of days.'

'Mick said that I wasn't to worry you with shop talk.'

'You'll worry me more if you don't tell me what's been going on. Are the stunt men still here?'

Rona shook her head. 'They couldn't stay. They went back to Melbourne to work on another project but they can come back after they finish that job.'

'I suppose it's better than having them on our payroll and doing nothing.'

'I thought that's what you'd say. Besides, it will take us a few days to line up some more tame buffaloes.'

Shan suppressed a shudder. 'No more animals with hang-ups, I hope.'

Rona grinned. 'Trust us to get the only neurotic buffalo in the whole Territory. The stockmen caught him after a while and now he's safely back in his pen at the wildlife park. The owners understood why we didn't want to risk using him again.'

'And what about the rest of the crew? Nobody's complaining about the hold-up, I hope?'

'N—no, nobody's complaining,' Rona said evasively.

'Not even Jason?'

'He's behaving like a lamb. I don't know what your King said to him but he's a changed man these days.'

'He's not "my" King,' Shan said irritably. She had the feeling there was something Rona was keeping from her. The change of subject had been too adroit for one thing. 'Is there anything else I should know about?' she asked.

Rona lowered her head and became very interested in the pattern on the bedspread. 'No, not a thing, everything's dandy,' she said without looking up.

'Rona . . .'

Her assistant jumped to her feet. 'I must be going. Mick said I wasn't to stay too long and tire you out.'

Before Shan could voice any more objections, Rona was gone. She stared after her thoughtfully. What was going on? It wasn't like Rona to be so secretive about anything. She debated whether to get up and go after her but her experimental attempt to sit up brought with it a wave of dizziness. Defeated, she sank back against the pillows. Whatever it was would have to wait until she felt up to dealing with it.

It was the next day before she felt up to going as far as her bathroom for a bath, far less anything more strenuous. Dr Spalding had allowed her to sit up in a chair for a while and she decided to freshen herself up, finding the sponge baths she'd been having inadequate.

As she waited for the vast tub to fill she remembered the time when King had shared it with her, arousing her to fever pitch with his touch. Easing her bruised but mending body into the bubbling water, she wondered where he was and what he was doing.

There had been no word from him since he left after his talk with Mick Spalding. If he had located Tammy, surely he would have called to let them know? Perhaps he was waiting until Shan and her crew had left before he returned. The thought that he would go to such lengths to avoid seeing her again was heartbreaking.

She would have to get used to it, she supposed. Since she couldn't tell him the truth about the baby for fear he would use it to pressure her into staying— or worse, to take the child from her as he had taken Tammy from Joanna—she would have to let him go on thinking the child belonged to another man.

Feeling better physically if not mentally, after her bath, she wrapped herself in a floral housecoat and wandered down to the living room where she found Rona and Dave deep in consultation.

Dave rose as she entered. 'Shan! You're looking wonderful—but should you be up and about so soon?'

'Thanks for the compliment, I didn't know a black eye did so much for my appearance,' she said drily, referring to the violet bruise which still darkened one cheekbone.

'I didn't mean that and you know it. Come and sit down before you fall down.'

She took his advice, sinking gratefully into an armchair. 'What are you two up to?'

Rona and Dave exchanged guilty glances. 'Uh, nothing. We were just going over the budget,' Rona said quickly.

'We were just about to drive over to the billabong for ... for a picnic,' Dave added, urging Rona to her feet.

'I got some magazines for you when I was in Katherine,' Rona said, handing them to her. 'We'll see you later.'

Then she was alone again clutching the glossy magazines Rona had thrust into her hands. She looked at them with distaste. Cookery and fashion were hardly her forté. She would have preferred a copy of *Variety* to catch up on industry gossip, but it probably wasn't obtainable in Katherine anyway.

Rona and Dave worried her with their hasty departure. She could have sworn they were discussing the film when she walked in, and the papers they had been pouring over looked more like a shooting script than a balance sheet. What were they up to?

She glanced at the clock. Only two in the afternoon. The hours stretched ahead endlessly before everyone would assemble for dinner and she could look forward to some lively conversation. Even Mrs Gordon had deserted her, having announced that she was attending a Country Women's Association get-together in Katherine. What was she going to do with herself for the rest of the day?

Shakily she got to her feet and tossed the magazines on to the sofa. She had had enough of being an invalid. She was determined to find out what Dave and Rona were up to. Why not follow them out to the billabong and find out?

The exertion involved in changing from her housecoat to jeans and a shirt almost made her change her mind. But she gritted her teeth and kept going, wincing as she bent double to tie her shoelaces.

Getting out to the billabong was less taxing although the bumpy drive along the rutted bush track did nothing for her bruises. 'Some picnic!' she muttered in astonishment, as she drove into the clearing beside the billabong.

The entire cast and crew except for Tammy were assembled there, all busy on their respective tasks. From where she sat, too stunned to move, she could see Dave directing Jason and some of the aboriginal actors in a scene which occurred after the buffalo charge in the script.

Professional discipline overcame curiosity and she sat still until Dave called 'cut', then she climbed stiffly out of the vehicle.

'Shan, what are you doing here?' he asked, catching sight of her.

'More to the point, what are you all doing here?'

'It was supposed to be a surprise for you,' Rona interrupted. 'Dave and I decided we could finish the location shooting ourselves while you were convalescing. You left pretty good notes, and you know I'm a frustrated producer so . . .'

She broke off as Shan enveloped her in a bear hug. 'I don't deserve you two,' she said, choking with emotion. 'I'm ashamed of all the things I suspected you of doing.'

'Knowing what nefarious types we are, your suspicions might have been well founded,' Dave joked. 'But as you can see, it was all above board.'

'How are you coping without Tammy?' Shan couldn't help asking.

A shadow passed across Dave's face, revealing how worried he was about the girl. 'We're shooting around her for the present,' he explained. 'Luckily, most of the remaining scenes don't involve her. Where she is seen from a distance, I've dressed her stand-in in her costume and filmed her from behind.'

'You've thought of everything,' Shan said in wonder. 'You've probably saved the picture from being a financial disaster.'

'Don't forget, we have a stake in it too,' Dave said awkwardly, moved by her response. 'We're really saving our own hides.'

She hugged him. 'I know, and I don't believe it for a minute, but if you say so . . .'

'What the devil do you think you're doing?'

She recoiled as the familiar voice barked behind her. 'King, you're back,' she said stupidly. 'I wasn't expecting you.'

'Obviously.' His voice was vibrant with anger. 'Get into the car.'

'But what's the . . .'

'There's no time. Just get in. I'll explain as we go.'

She shook her head decisively. 'I'm not going anywhere until you tell me what's going on.'

Unconsciously, she planted her feet wide apart, bracing her hands on her hips to emphasise her new-found defiance.

His eyes blazed and his cheeks flushed. He looked as if he was about to explode. Then he took a deep breath and let it out slowly. 'Very well. Tammy's convinced she killed you. After leading me on a wild goose chase for two days, she barricaded herself into the old homestead, refusing to come out until she sees you for herself. She's got my old double barrelled shotgun with her.'

Shan's fingers flew to her mouth. 'Oh my God!'

'*Now* will you come?'

'Of course.' Even as she spoke, she was hurrying towards his Land-Rover. Behind her, she heard Dave's exclamation of horror. 'I'll follow you over there.'

'Take my jeep,' Shan called to him as King jumped in beside her. The car jolted forwards and she sagged in her seat. With King's announcement had gone what little strength she had mustered to come out here and now she felt as if her limbs were made of jelly. 'I think I'm going to be ill,' she said urgently.

'Can't stop,' he said through clenched teeth. 'You'll just have to hang on.'

His lack of concern made her furiously angry, overcoming her nausea. Tammy was all that mattered, as usual. Never mind what Shan thought or felt. At the same time, she realised she was being selfish. Despite their differences, she didn't want Tammy to get hurt. The thought of the teenager locked up in the old homestead with King's shotgun sent a chill down her spine. What if they couldn't convince her to come out? 'How much farther?' she asked.

He spared her a quick sideways glance. 'Just a couple of miles. Are you all right?'

Tears pricked the backs of her eyes at the sudden switch in his tone. 'I'm okay.'

'Good girl.' He turned his attention back to the road which was no more than twin tracks through the grassy savannah plain.

Just when she thought they would never reach their destination, the wide verandahs of the old homestead came into sight. The door was closed and the windows were shuttered. There was no sign of life.

As soon as he brought the jeep to a halt, King leapt out and strode towards the building. 'Are you there, Tammy? I've brought Shan with me.'

'You can't have. She's dead. I killed her,' came the muffled response.

'No, you didn't. I'm very much alive. See for yourself,' Shan called back, walking up behind King.

For a moment, she thought Tammy might refuse to look outside, then one of the shutters lurched outwards and Tammy's face, dusty and tear-streaked, appeared in the opening. 'Shan—is it really you?'

Shan spread her arms wide. 'Cross my heart.'

'But the buffalo ran right over you.'

'Maybe that's how it looked from a distance but your father pushed me out of the way. I was only grazed in passing.'

After a few minutes of strained silence, the door creaked open and Tammy hurtled herself into King's arms, sobbing uncontrollably. 'Dad, I'm so sorry. Can you ever forgive me?'

He held her at arm's length. 'Shan is the one you should apologise to.'

Tammy looked down at the ground and drew circles in the powdery dust with her shoe. 'I'm sorry, Shan,' she said in barely audible tones. 'I didn't want you to get hurt, only to get a fright. I never dreamed the buffalo would break the gate down and charge you.'

Shan made no attempt to disguise her horror. 'But why do such a thing at all, Tammy? Do you hate me that much.'

When Tammy's silence continued, King's expression hardened. 'Shan asked you a question, young lady. I think you owe her an answer.'

'Why should I? She's not my mother!'

'That's enough!' Before Shan could react, King's hand whipped out and caught Tammy a stinging blow across her cheek. The imprint of his fingers stood out angrily against her white skin. She could only stare at him, shocked.

'King, don't!' Shan cried.

His massive chest heaved as he fought himself. 'I'm sorry I lost control and hit you, Tammy. But I won't have you speaking to Shan like that.'

Once, she had begged him to defend her against Tammy but not with violence, and not now when it was too late. 'I don't want to come between you two like this,' she agonised. 'I know I'm not your mother, Tammy. She was special to you and . . .'

'She wasn't,' hissed Tammy, one hand clutching her stinging cheek. 'I hated her.'

Shan and King exchanged startled looks. 'What?'

'You heard me. I hated her. Oh, she was a great actress of course, but she was a terrible person. Can't you see—I'm her daughter. I don't want to grow up like her, hated by everybody.'

'It doesn't have to be that way.' Shan's head was spinning with the unexpectedness of Tammy's response.

'Yes it does. I have the acting bug like her. I have her temper. Everything will be the same for me, I just know it will.'

'But you wanted to live with your mother.'

'It was better than inflicting myself on someone else, since I had her rotten genes anyway.'

'You also have mine,' King reminded her. 'But I still don't see what this has to do with Shan?'

Tammy hunched her shoulders and half-turned away. 'When you came to Faraway, it was just too good to be true. I knew something was bound to go wrong. It's the story of my life.'

'So you decided to burst the bubble before someone else could do it for you?'

The truth was becoming painfully clear. Tammy was so convinced that bad blood would out that she couldn't see any other future for herself than to follow in her mother's footsteps. From King's brooding expression she guessed he was reaching the same conclusion.

'Why didn't you tell us how you felt?' he asked.

'I didn't think you'd understand.'

'You didn't give us much chance,' King observed. 'You were so anxious to hurt Shan before she could hurt you that you didn't stop to think she might be able to help you.'

Shan laid a hand on his arm. 'Don't be too hard on her. This can't be easy for her to face.'

'It hasn't exactly been easy for any of us.'

'I said I'm sorry,' Tammy said tearfully, looking very young and frightened by the cold fury in her father's voice.

He was too angry to be diverted. 'You think sorry is adequate after the way you've behaved, my girl, but I don't. For one thing, there's the matter of that letter you forged to get Shan to come here, and the one Jason Cody tells me you cooked up for him. You can go to gaol for that, you know.'

Shan blanched and gripped his arm harder. 'King! You're terrifying the poor child.'

'She's not a child and it's time she understood the consequences of her actions—damn it, she nearly got you killed.'

Shan shuddered at the memory. 'I accept her word that she didn't mean things to go that far. And I think she knows better than to try forgery again, don't you, Tammy?'

Tammy flashed her a look of surprise mixed with gratitude. 'You can send me to prison and I know I deserve it, but I can't be any sorrier than I am now that I tried to hurt you, Shan. I guess I just couldn't believe you wanted someone like me around.'

Shan smiled through the tears which blurred her

vision. 'That's enough talk about prison. I'm willing to accept your word of honour that you won't do such things ever again. Won't we, King?' She included him, fearful that he would carry out his threat to hand Tammy over to the law.

He was silent for a long time, massaging his shadowed chin with one hand. 'If it's what you want, I'll go along,' he said at last. 'But make no mistake, Tammy, one step out of line and I'll see that you're dealt with just like any other young criminal. Is that clear?'

White-faced, Tammy nodded. 'I understand.'

There was a screech of tyres and Dave's jeep pulled up, sending up clouds of choking dust. He jumped out, his anxiety noticeably lessening as he caught sight of Tammy standing between Shan and King. 'I had a flat tyre,' he apologised. 'But it looks like I needn't have hurried.'

'As a matter of fact, you're just in time to take Tammy back to the house,' King told him. 'Oh, and you'd better take my shotgun with you. It's in the homestead.'

'It isn't loaded,' Tammy admitted sheepishly. She fetched the weapon and handed it to Dave then the two of them climbed into his jeep and drove off.

'Will she be all right?' Shan asked anxiously, watching them go.

'I'll have a talk to the doctor who treated her before, but after what we've discovered today, I don't think she'll need much more medical help. Now we've finally gotten to the root of her problem, maybe she won't be so afraid of growing up.'

At least some good would come of her presence here, Shan thought. The future looked much brighter for King and Tammy, even if it was too late for Shan. Wearily, she passed a hand over her eyes, bringing King swiftly to her side.

'Are you all right?'

'I'm very tired. Can we go back to Faraway now?'

He scooped her up in muscular arms and held her close against his chest. Lacking the strength to resist, she let her head drop against him and breathed in the comforting male scent of him. It was probably for the last time anyway.

A sense of loss assailed her as he settled her on the passenger's seat and moved around to the driver's side. If only they had known sooner how Tammy felt, there might have been a chance for Shan and King. But it was too late now. He believed she was pregnant by another man.

She looked around in surprise as King steered the car off the track to the homestead, in favour of another little-used one. 'Where are we going?'

'You'll see in a few minutes.'

There was an air of suppressed excitement about him which hadn't been there until now. Of course, he was relieved about Tammy but it didn't explain this crazy detour. 'I'd really rather go back,' she said tiredly.

'Soon. We're going to have a talk first. You aren't getting away from me this time.'

If he wanted to berate her for having a baby by another man, he was going about it in a very strange way. But before she could ask any more questions he swung the car into a small grassy clearing edged by pandanus palms, leading down to a narrow band of golden sand and a sparkling waterhole beyond. The water's edge was thick with flowering lilies and a family of cranes picked their long-legged way through the roots in search of fish and frogs. 'Our waterhole,' she breathed.

'Yes, ours. It seems like the right place for us to find ourselves again—the you and I, we managed to lose during our stormy marriage.'

What was he talking about? Why had he brought her to this waterhole—the same one where she had swum naked while he photographed her, calling her his wood nymph. 'I don't understand,' she protested.

'You will.'

He parked a short distance from the water's edge and got out, retrieving a checked travel rug from the back seat. After spreading it on the ground beside the car, he helped her out and settled her on the rug with her back braced against a wheel. 'Comfy?'

'Fine thanks.' Remembering her recent ordeal, she glanced around nervously but there were no buffaloes to be seen.

He sensed her fear. 'Just let a buffalo come anywhere near my wife!'

She sighed. 'Don't you think you should stop this "wife" business now?'

'It would be a shame, since I'm finally getting the hang of it.'

'What?'

He plucked a few strands of the long grass and twisted them between his fingers. 'Hell, Shan, you said the Cattle King never makes mistakes, but I made a beauty when I let you go. I don't want to make that mistake again.'

'If it's because of the baby . . .'

'No, it isn't that, although I'm thrilled with the news.'

Her eyes widened in amazement. 'You're pleased?'

'Of course. You may have convinced Mick Spalding that the baby isn't mine, but you'll never convince me.'

'How can you be so sure?'

'Because despite what you think I trust you. I know I accused you of seeing Dave and Jason but that was my jealousy talking. I know you would never give yourself to another man while you're still my wife.'

He knew her better than she suspected. 'All right, the child is yours—but you aren't going to use it to keep me here. I'll fight you through every court in the land if I have to.'

'There's no need. If you still want to leave, I shan't stop you, although I hope you'll let me take care of all the baby's expenses. I love you too much to keep you against your will.'

She was hearing things, she must be. 'Say that again,' she demanded.

'I said I won't keep you here.'

'No, the other part.'

'That I love you? You must believe me, I do, but I'll understand if you despise me after everything that's happened.'

'I wouldn't know how,' she denied. 'I was afraid you'd only want me to stay because of the baby.'

His gaze became caressing. 'There's only one reason why I want you to stay and that's because I can't live without you. But this time, I want our marriage to be perfect. With Tammy going to drama school in Sydney soon, we'll have Faraway all to ourselves.'

'As long as she understands that this is still her home and she's always welcome here,' Shan said firmly, not wanting any misunderstandings this time. 'At least in Sydney she'll have Dave to take care of her.'

'I'm counting on it. Dave's love will do more than anything else to restore her confidence in herself.'

'I'm sure of it. When you set Dave up in his own studio, they'll be working together as well, so Tammy need never feel inadequate again.'

He dropped down on to the rug beside her. 'Who says I'm setting Dave up in a studio?'

'Tammy said you plan to finance more pictures after *Call of the Outback* is released.'

'So I do, but not for Dave. He's quite capable of making it on his own. And as for Tammy, I have to get used to letting her stand on her own feet. That was another of my mistakes, encouraging her to rely on me instead of herself.'

'But she said you're in favour of a husband producing pictures for his wife,' Shan said, confused.

'I presume you don't mind this husband backing pictures for this wife?'

She could hardly believe her ears. Why hadn't she thought of that? She had been so sure that King's plans were for Tammy that she hadn't given a thought to herself. 'Will you mind me working?' she asked uncertainly, remembering his earlier objections. 'I mean, when the baby is old enough.'

'I'll be jealous as hell. But Tammy wasn't the only one hiding from the truth. I had to face the fact that the film world didn't take Joanna away from me. I never had her in the first place. She would have gone her own way no matter what job she held so I can't blame an entire industry because I wasn't husband enough to hold her.'

'You can't blame yourself either. You just said the flaw was in her, not in anything you did.'

He frowned. 'You're letting me off too lightly. I've put you through hell since we met, because I wouldn't believe that Tammy had a problem. Can't you at least yell at me or something?'

'I could beat you,' she said impishly, leaning closer so her lips grazed his cheek. 'Take that.' She kissed him again. 'And that.'

Before she could pounce again, his mouth trapped hers in a kiss which was as fiery and possessive as any brand. His hand, warm and strong, slid inside her blouse and he pulled her hard against him. She linked her arms around his neck and urged his head down as if to draw his very essence into herself with his kiss. A throbbing ache started up deep within her but she quieted it, knowing they had a lifetime to assuage their need for each other.

From beyond the pandanus palms, a solitary buffalo wandered into the clearing, watching them with quiet incurious eyes. It stood its ground for a moment then ambled off into the scrub. Safe in the all-consuming passion of King's embrace, Shan didn't even notice.

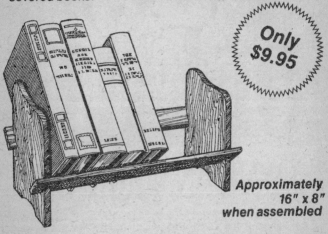

Shay Flanagan is Gypsy,
the raven-haired beauty who inflamed passion
in the hearts of two Falconer men.

Carole Mortimer

GYPSY

Lyon Falconer, a law unto himself, claimed Shay—when he didn't have the right. Ricky Falconer, gentle and loving married Shay—when she had no other choice.

Now her husband's death brings Shay back within Lyon's grasp. Once and for all Lyon intends to prove that Shay has always been—will always be—*his* Gypsy!